YOU AND I

YOU AND I

EROTIC LESBIAN SHORT STORIES

Raven Elizabeth

To order additional copies of this book, contact:
Xlibris
1-888-795-4274
www.Xlibris.com
Orders@Xlibris.com
794400

To all the wonderful ladies in my life who both inspired and supported me in my writing endeavors, I hope you enjoy what you have helped me bring to life. A special acknowledgment goes out to the few exceptional women who believe in me enough to encourage me to follow my dreams.

CONTENTS

UNCHAINED PASSION

It's a week before I'm to return home. As usual, we have been constantly texting and talking on the phone whenever possible. Unfortunately, I've been a little busy wrapping up post deployment things. Almost every night we Skype before I go to bed. But not tonight. Today I have been very busy and haven't been able to text you very often. I can feel you are a little disappointed through the text messages you are sending. I try to apologize to you as best I can, but you don't seem to believe me.

It's Friday, so I know I only have a limited time to really have a conversation with you before you meet up with your friends. I wish I could just calm you down by wrapping my arms around you and kissing you, but I'm too far yet for my arms to be able to reach you. Needless to say, I'm unable to help you find peace before you go out.

I text you my wishes and love around 7:30 p.m. your time. You don't text me back. You go off to your friend's house, frustrated and disappointed, so of course, when you get to your friend's house, you vent and drink. Then you all head down to Hour Place, the local gay bar, to watch the drag show and dance.

When you get to the bar, you see a lot of my friends there. You say "Hi," then think nothing of it. The drag show seems to have a theme tonight. All the performers have masquerade masks on. The bar is dark and getting packed. You and your friends find a table up front so you can enjoy the show.

The music quickly changes over to the intro song for Nix, the reigning empress. She is looking very regal in her gown and mask. She goes into her usual updates and upcoming events, then introduces her first performer. The first queen comes out with extreme energy and gets the crowd riled up. Everyone seems to be having a great time. Then Nix introduces a drag king. No one knows this one, so you can tell the whole crowd is just waiting to see what "he" can do.

"His" music starts to pound, and "his" hips begin to move. The music is very erotic, and everyone responds to the combination. Since everyone is wearing some sort of masks, the show is more of a dance performance. You seem to follow his hips across the dance floor, like you're hypnotized. Then out of nowhere, the performer rips his shirt off, exposing her abs, hips, and wrapped breasts. Your eyes trace the defined lines of her body as she grinds her hips with the air and the patrons giving her tips. You can't help yourself, so you hop off your seat and head down to the dance floor with your dollar in hand.

You expect her to just take the money or even grind a little with you. Instead, she pulls you further onto the dance floor and grinds hard into you. You find yourself following suit and forgetting about everyone else around you. It's been a long time since you have danced so helplessly with someone like that. Then the song ends, and you slowly make your way back to your table. Before she totally lets go of you, she traces your hips with her hands. You catch your breath for a second as you find your seat.

You and your friends share a look then smile and laugh. The show continues on in front of you, but there is just something about that performer that won't let you think of anything or anyone else. You watch her in the bar area, just trying to build up the courage to say "Hi," but all you can manage to do is smile. She catches you looking and gives you a very manly nod. You just smile bigger, deeper.

Nix comes over the microphone and says they are taking a little break, so you take advantage and run to the restroom. What you don't see is the performer follows right behind you. You come out of the stall to her looking at you, but she still has her mask on, so you can't tell for sure. She takes you by the hips and pushes you back into the large stall. She turns your back to her and lets her hands slide from your hips to other places. You whisper you can't, you shouldn't, but her hands carry a familiar heat and weight to them. They comfort you.

Quickly she has your legs spread. You're breathing like you could cum with just a thought. She wraps one arm over your shoulder and in front of your throat. You brace yourself with one hand on the closest wall and the other on her hip. Then she moves her unburdened hand between your skin and your underwear. There is something about her fingers that begs you to let go. Before she even has a chance to enter you, you freeze. She knows you know.

She leans into your ear, tightening her grip around your neck. Your breathing becomes very rapid. Your heart pounds in the back of your throat. You feel the heat of her breath on your neck and ear. She presses her body firmly against your ass. Then you hear it—my deep and husky voice reaches you as I thrust my fingers past your grip and deep inside of you. "Missed me that much, did you?" I thrive on how wet I've make you. You loudly moan as you reach up and grab my hair. Your hips work around my fingers, and within seconds, I feel you cuming for me. Unable to just let you off with just one, my fingers begin working relentlessly inside of your amazingly wet, tight pussy. You spasm repeatedly around my finger. "I've missed you that much too, baby!"

I wrap my arm around your waist and slowly begin to remove my fingers from inside of you. You take your hand and undo your pants, easing the pressure around my hand. Once my hand is free, I lift my mask and clean my fingers. (Oh god, the way you smell and taste drives me crazy. Mmmmm, yes, please, I'll take seconds, and thirds!) I tenderly trace my lips down your neckline to your shoulder. Your knees begin to fail you. I hold you tight.

I feel you collect yourself, then you spin on me. Now I'm the one caught off guard. You kneel in front of me knowing how wet I'd be for you; how wet you make me when you cum. You look up into my eyes as your hands work on removing my belt and my pants. Your hands work their way around and over my hips. You know just how to tease me. My breathing becomes very erratic and heavy. I watch your lips move to meet my navel. Your fingers trace over my hip bones in my boxer's waistband. Your lips begin making their way down my body, following my underwear. Halfway down, you quickly rip my boxers down to my ankles. I watch your tongue play over my clit, teasing me. Then, as if you are just waiting for me to exhale, you wrap your lips around my clit, sucking hard and caressing it with your tongue. I want to scream. Holy fuck, baby, you're gonna make me cum before I can even fully enjoy your tongue, but I don't. I can't. I can't even moan. All I can manage to do is not lose my balance.

Within a minute or so, I find myself gripping the back of your head and hold you hard into me. I need more, I want more. (Fuck! Don't scream.) I cum all over your chin and lips. You force me to take every sensitive movement of your tongue. I must force you to stop. I have to force myself to breathe again.

Realizing we are running out of time, I pull you to your feet to face me. You're breathless and breathtaking. As the tears run down your eyes, I wipe them away and caress your face as I move in to kiss you. You slap me. You call me an ass. Then you kiss me like you're gonna lose yourself. (I could lose myself in you!)

I break our kiss to get cleaned up, watching you in the mirror. I tell you how I have another performance before I can be yours. You just watch me. "I'll see you out there," I say as I lower my mask over my face and walk out of the bathroom, leaving you speechless.

You move to the sink and catch your breath, still reeling from what just happened. As you retouch on your makeup, one of your friends comes in and ask you about what happened. She saw that you were followed. You just smile. You can't stop smiling. You make your way back to your seat, still smiling from ear to ear. My friends see you and give you a questioning look. That's when you realize I'm not only for your surprise; I'm also theirs.

The music changes again, and you sit eagerly, awaiting my next song. The soft piano plays in your head. "Wanted" is playing. I come out in a tux. I grab Chelsea and give her a dance, then I move to Jasmin. You know the song is a chorus away from ending, and you start to think I won't dance with you. I make my way around the crowd, finally coming up behind you and pull you to your feet and out onto the dance floor. I twirl you around like a princess, then I pull you in close. The music slows for the last verse, and we go slow with it. I gently push you away and drop to my knee. Without removing my mask, I pull out your ring and just look at you. You meet my eyes and start crying as you continuously nod yes. I slip the ring on your finger as the song's last note is played.

I stand up and walk you to your table. I sit you down and just hold you. Everyone around us just stares at us. Half of the crowd knows you, and the other half know me. I hold you tight and ask you gently if I can let you go for a second so I can remove my mask and answer all the questioning looks. You just nod. I take a step back, and slowly, I look at the crowd as I remove my mask. I quickly turn to Nix and give her a nod and mouth, "Thank you." Both my friends and your friends' jaws have hit the floor.

I just give your friends a wink and smile at mine and wait to get swarmed. I wrap my arms around you once more, and you pull me so tight against you that I don't think we are two people anymore. I manage to reach into my breast pocket and pull out my handkerchief for you to wipe your tears. I kiss your head softly and smile. Then we get swarmed. Everyone gives us hugs and congratulates us. I barely hear any of it. I'm just lost in the bliss of holding you. "I LOVE YOU, BABY GIRL!" You look up at me and give me that amazing smile of yours.

Then Nix comes to the speakers and breaks the serenity that I just found again. She says it's time to celebrate, and I for one can't think of a better thing to do in this moment. I quickly pull you to your feet and onto the dance floor. We spend the next hour or so dancing and having fun with our friends. Then I whisper in your ear, "I wanna take you home now and make love to you! I need you naked in my arms!" You just look at me with those smoldering eyes and smile. I take your hand and lead you through the crowd. You gather your things and say good night to your friends, and I do the same.

You walk me to your car because I showed up in a cab. You hand over the keys to let me drive. I open the door for you, then I run around to my side and climb in. I don't even have a chance to start the car before you lean over and kiss me. Your intensity hits me like the freight train going behind us. I can't get enough of you. I instantly undo your pants and slide my way between your now soaked underwear and your throbbing mound. You pull your pants down past your knees, so I have a full range of motion. You toss your head back in a spasm and moan as I coerce the first of many orgasms from you. You try to force my fingers out of you, but I refuse to quit. (I WANT MORE!) So you take it upon yourself to slide your hand in my boxers to tease my throbbing, soaking wet pussy. I don't stop till I feel your body contract once more around my quickening fingers. This time, your body grips me so hard I can't even move my fingers as your cum washes over them. Your whole body stiffens. Your hand presses hard against my clit, and the slight shutters that ripple through your body reach me at my pinnacle. I can't help myself; my body takes over my thoughts and begins to orgasm as yours ends. Your fingers, since my impending explosion, begin moving over my clit again, hard. I catch my breath for a split second, then I hand myself over to the pleasure you're forcing from my pussy. I scream, "Holy fuck, baby, don't STOP! Please don't STOP!"

(Holy fuck!) "God, how I've missed you, baby!" I say with a dimpled smile. You lean over and kiss me tenderly with the love I've been missing. When you pull your lips away from mine, I see you smile and bite your lip. Knowing what you're thinking, I slowly remove my fingers from the warmth we created between your legs. You, on the other hand, decide that I need a little more teasing, and you keep your hand in my pants as long as possible.

I start the car up, trying to focus on what I need to do to get us to bed as quickly and safely as I can. I widen my legs, giving you more access. You take your other hand and unzip my pants so you can have more free range. (Time to practice my multitasking skills! God, how you make it difficult to concentrate!) I start down the road, and we head to my hotel. After I miss the turn, you think I should have just taken the road back to your house, but I tell you to just enjoy the ride. A minute later, I pull into the Davenport Hotel. You quickly remove your hand from my pants, which makes me catch my breath. You give me a quick look of "wow" and "really?" wrapped in a smile.

I move quickly to pull up my pants before the valet gets to your door. I just smile my cocky smile. We both get out, and I give him my keys and grab your hand and lead you to my room. I can feel your pulse racing through your hand. As we walk up to the room you ask me how long I've been planning this. I just look at you and simply say, "Since the day I left you." Then we arrive at my room. I open the door and let you in ahead of me so you can see the room before I help you destroy it.

The bed has rose petals covering it, with white lilies on either side and candles burning on every surface. I give you a second, then step behind you, slowly moving my hands down your shoulders to your hands. I kiss you softly behind your ear, lulling you into a sense of relaxation before I make your breathing catch. You lean back into me, wanting more. Lucky for me, you stop right next to a wall. I spin you around to face me and aggressively press you to the wall as my lips meet yours. I can feel your breathing stop. I grip your hip hard and twine my fingers in your hair, pulling your lips from mine, slowly. I bite your lower lip before you get the chance to. I'm hungry. Hungry for you. Hungry for your touch, for your raw passion, for the taste of you.

You expose your neck to me willingly. The heat of my tongue warms you straight down between your lips. My lips are greedy to take the taste of you in. I kiss every inch of your neck, teasing your shoulders with my teeth. I find the spot just above your shoulder and sink my teeth in aggressively, but not hard. I give you a moment to catch your breath. Your hands are up against the wall in complete surrender. Releasing my grip on your hair and hip, I take my hands around the collar of your shirt, tracing your collarbone for a moment. Then in one quick, decisive movement, I rip your shirt in half, exposing your breasts, barely covered by your strapless black bra. You gasp in shock of my movements. I take one hand and make quick work of your bra, dropping it at your feet. My mouth hungrily wraps around a nipple, and gently, I begin to suck and nibble. Your hands fall to my shoulders and begin undressing me.

I work with you, allowing my clothes to pile around our feet. My hands roam all over your body, remembering your curves and linger spots. I work my lips down your naked body. Your hands find their way to my shoulders. You dig your nails in as my teeth find your hips, grazing along your bones as they dip towards the heat radiating from between your legs. (I can't help myself. I want to take you hard and fast, but I want to enjoy your body. Mmmmm, but that smell . . .) I stop myself from teasing you and force your legs out a step and wide. I hook one of your legs around my shoulder to drape over my back, and without warning, I dive in. (I need that taste on my tongue. I need to taste you. I need to make you cum on my face, on my tongue!)

"Oh, baby, mmm. Oh . . . yes" is all I heard. Your nails dig deep in my shoulder and now the back of my head. You rock your hips into me, begging for more. I don't stop. I make you cum for me. You try to pull my head from between your legs, but I just tighten my grip on your leg over my back and take my other hand and trace it up the back of your other leg, under your left ass cheek, and between your lips. My fingers dive right into your expectant, hungry pussy. Within seconds, your breathing quickens and becomes labored. I begin moaning over your clit, sending vibrations throughout your pussy. It doesn't take much now. Your hips start thrusting hard. I steady my back, preparing for your eventual collapse. I start drumming my fingers inside of you. I feel the weight of your body weigh on me more. Your thighs tighten around my head, and you clamp down on my fingers as explosions ring from the top of your head to the back of your throat, to the butterflies in your stomach, to the tips of your toes and back to where my tongue awaits for your taste to melt me. "Mmmmm, aaaaah . . . aaaaah, hmmm" is all I hear. I gently withdraw my fingers, bringing them one at a time to my lips. "Mmmmm, you taste soooo good, baby!" I say as I look up to you. I drop my shoulder and allow your leg to fall to the ground as I catch you sliding down the wall.

I hold you tight against my naked chest, enjoying the extreme bliss of being able to wrap my arms around you and the pleasing sensation you have brought me. Your heart pounds audibly. I kiss your forehead and pull you closer. "I'm never letting you go again, baby!" I whisper. All I hear in return is mumbling. I pull back just enough to see you crying. "Shh, baby, why are you crying?" You just shake your head slightly. I kiss you and just hold you close. I help you up to your feet after a few minutes and walk you over to the bed. I lay you on top of the rose petals, then leave you to use the restroom because, well, you know how wet I get when I make you cum. When I return, I bring you a glass of water and some tissue, just in case. But when I turn the corner, I find you passed out and spread eagle on the bed.

I drink the water, then take a shower, giving you a little time to sleep. I was thinking I'd just climb in bed with you and just cuddle, but something in me wasn't satisfied yet. So I towel off and wrap the towel around my waist. I come out of the bathroom to find you in the same position I left you in, which works out perfect for what I have planned for you. I walk to the end of the bed between your legs. I slowly lie down between your thighs, placing my hands around each hip. I lean my head gently down to kiss your lips. My shoulders slowly spread your legs farther apart, separating your legs and exposing your clit.

You are still sleeping, so I take my tongue and flatten it as I lower it onto your sensitive clit. I apply more and more pressure as I dip down towards your hole. I'm not quite sure of how you're going to react to this, so I grip your hips firmly. I take my tongue and slide it inside of you, taking my lips and wrapping them around your clit and my tongue. On about the third penetrating movement, you begin to stir. You moan as you cum. That lit an extra fire in me that I need to really take you in. I pull my tongue out and drag it back up to your clit. My lips create a seal around my tongue and your clit and begin sucking as my tongue flicks and circles. I know exactly when you fully wake up and realize you aren't dreaming because your hands fly to the back of my head and shoulder and you dig in. Your hips flex upwards, demanding more.

I take my hand from your hip and circle your leg to the crease of the soft skin between your hip and mound. I gently stroke the area, teasing you till you verbally beg me to penetrate you. (I want to hear how much you want me inside of you, how much you want me to take you and make you cum.) I take the back of my fingers and drag them towards your wanting hole. I take my fingers and tilt them upwards and apply pressure to the lower art of your opening as I move inside you at an angle. The tips of my fingers catch the sensitive skin just behind your clit, creating an amazing mixture of pressure and pleasure. My fingers complement your hip movements. The quicker your hips move, the quicker my fingers move. And you figured that out fast. My tongue on the other hand is going at its own tempo. But the combination of all the sensations is about to throw you over the edge. Knowing your body the way I do, I sense the impending explosion of passion. I release your hip with my other hand and reach for your luscious nipple. I palm your breast and start stimulating your nipple, effectively snapping the last straw. Your hips spasm rapidly beneath me, causing my fingers to be rapid, extending out your orgasm. I only stop because you start to crawl away from me. I just can't get enough of you!

I don't know what to expect now, but I definitely don't expect you to do what comes next.

Before I even know what is happening you lean up, grab me under my arms and haul me up on the bed, out of my towel, and flip me on my back. You straddle me and pin me to the bed in a single move. I feel your wetness rubbing against my overly pounding, throbbing mound. You begin grinding your wetness into mine. (God, I'm soaking wet and you haven't even really touched me yet.) You lean down and begin kissing me all over, on my eye lids, my cheeks, and my lips. You softly tease my lips with yours. I feel your breath warm my skin, and it sends shivers down my spine to my pussy. You forcefully make your way around my neck, kissing and sucking. You stop to nibble behind my ear. Then I feel you readjust your position over me, spreading my lips with your thigh. "Oh, baby, don't stop. Your body feels so good! I need you! Tease me, please me, do what you will to me, just don't stop!"

You grind into me, applying just the right amount of pressure. (If you keep moving like that, I'm gonna cum before I even get to enjoy what you're gonna do to me!) You move your hips all around, hitting every sensitive spot I have. Then for some reason, you pause. You take your teeth and dig them into my shoulder, and at the same time, you resume pressing your hip into my clit. "Oooohhhh, baby . . . mmmm. Put your fingers inside of me. I want to feel you inside me. I NEED to feel you inside of me. Please!" And with that, you lick between your teeth as you release your grip. I feel your hands release my arms. You work your way down my body with your tongue and hands. You tease my nipples and nibble on my hips.

My hips begin grinding in anticipation of your fingers. I take my hands and scoop up your hair, revealing your hungry eyes burning into me. You watch me watching you. (FUCK, YOU ARE SO HOT!) You take a hand between our bodies and slide your fingers deep inside of me, curling them at the perfect moment. A moan escapes from deep within me. With that, you dive down between my thighs and encase my clit in your hot mouth. The heat of your tongue starts to bring me to my breaking point. You pin my hip down with your arm and circle my hardened clit. (Fuck me, I'm gonna cum all over you!) Then you just raise your head and start climbing back up my body as your fingers thrust in and out of my tightening pussy. You attack my lips, taking my breath away once more.

Out of nowhere, I feel your thumb begin to circle my clit, then the circles become smaller and smaller. As the circles shrink, you apply more and more pressure. (Holy crap, I'm gonna cum.) Your fingers start pulsing under my clit inside of me. God, all the sensations. I pull away from your lips just long enough to whisper, "I'm gonna cum, baby, don't stop!" You kiss me with so much unchained passion that it puts me over the edge. I grips and spasms around your fingers. My back arches and my hips slam into you. You just intensify your fingers inside of me. I feel like my heart is in my throat. I can't cum hard enough. I can't breathe. (Holy fuck, did I need you.) Then one at a time, you stop your movements. First your fingers and thumb, then your hips and lips. You just stop and look at me. A tear falls helplessly down my cheek as I smile and pull you back down on top of me, kissing you. (You look soooo amazing in candlelight!)

ROAD TRIP

We are driving on our way to the Oregon Coast, and once again, you are the one driving, and I am lying back in the passenger seat. I know how much you love to be in control. We've been flirting all day, building the sexual tension between us. It's only a couple of hours into the trip. the scenery has become redundant and I'm horny, so I begin to touch myself.

At first, I look over at you while my hand begins moving up and down over my mound, but after a few seconds of touching myself, I close my eyes and enjoy the sensation overcoming my body. I feel you take your eyes off the road to see what I'm doing. You notice that my eyes are closed, and my breath is deepening. You can't stop watching me, waiting to see if I'll stop or open my eyes to see you watching me, but I don't. I keep going. My hips begin moving under my hand. My breathing becomes louder.

You turn your eyes back to the road, trying to focus on your driving. Your pulse has quickened in response to the excitement running through your mind and in the seat next to you. It almost becomes too much for you, knowing that I'm touching myself next to you.

You reach a hand over, sliding it over the top of my thigh up to the back of my hand. My hand freezes. You press my hand hard against my pussy. You can feel the throbbing of my clit through my jeans.

Our hands begin moving as one, stroking me. You take my hand deep between my legs, pushing my fingers inward, and then upward over my now hardened clit.

We stroke my pussy as you try to multitask. You begin to feel the heat grow between my legs. You push my hand aside and unbutton my pants. The excitement has overcome you, and you can't take it anymore—you have to be inside of me.

I open my eyes and look at you. I wait for you to touch me. I pull my pants and boxers down past my knees to show you how much I need you to touch me.

You look into my eyes for a moment, giving me that smirk of knowing, then you slide your hand down my inner thigh and onto my wet pussy. Your fingers slip between my engorged lips easily. You stoke my clit and press your palm on the top of my mound. I begin moaning, gripping the seat under me with my right hand, and your leg with my left.

(God, the touch of your fingers feels so GOOD!)

My heart is racing, and my breathing is heavy. I turn my head towards you, "Don't stop! I want you to make me cum! I want to cum all over you!"

By now, you're breathing has deepened. Your pulse is coming harder and faster against my clit. You smile at me as your hand quickens. Your fingers press deep inside of me, drumming against my internal G-spot.

You move your palm in circular motions against my clit while your fingers flutter inside of me. My adrenaline rushes, and my legs begin to tingle. I can feel my body tense.

It doesn't take long before I start coming all over your fingers. My legs flex and my hands tear at the seat below me. "Oh god, don't stop! Fuck me . . . oh yes, YES!"

My words trail off as I become breathless and can't take it anymore. I look at you and give you a satisfied smile. I tap your leg and breathlessly whisper, "Okay, okay. I give in! I can't take it anymore."

You look at me and smile. You slowly withdraw your wet fingers from inside of me. I take a second to compose myself, then I pull up my boxers and pants.

I open the glove box, looking for some napkins for you. Finding some, I grab them and turn to you. You look at me and begin cleaning your fingers with your tongue. I watch your tongue glide around and between each finger. Then you slide your fingers deep into your mouth, dragging them seductively in and out.

When you've sufficiently cleaned your fingers, you slide them from between your lips, smirking at me. I begin smiling and hand you a napkin. You take them from me and dry your hand. I notice a rest stop ahead and ask you to pull in.

The place looks deserted and the parking lot is empty. I walk to the bathroom and check the doors. Finding one unlocked, I push it open and walk in. You follow shortly after me and enter as I finish cleaning up. Your footsteps echo past me as you go into the largest stall at the end.

I walk out of my stall and wash my hands. As I'm drying my hands, I hear you flush the toilet, so I walk towards your stall. (I need to fuck you!) I hear the slide of the lock as you unlatch it. I grab you as the door swings opens. I take your breath away, kissing you hard as I push you back into the stall.

Pressing your body against the wall, I take a hand down and over your breast. I grip it aggressively and then release it as my hand trails down over your navel to the crotch of your pants. I entangle my other hand in your hair at the top of your neck. Your breathing is becoming deep and sporadic as I begin rubbing my hand over your pussy and kissing your cheek down to your neck.

You plead for me to take your pants off. I just continue teasing you for a moment, rubbing between your legs with the palm of my hand. Once I feel you can't take it anymore, I drop my hand from your hair and rip open your pants. I force them along with your soaked, black silk underwear to your ankles.

I take one hand up your inner thigh past your wet lips and press my finders deep inside of your pussy. My palm presses against your clit, massaging it.

I kiss your neck and whisper, "I want to feel you cum! I want to taste you!"

You start moving your hips to the rhythm of my fingers inside of you. I kiss you down your body. "Eat my pussy!" is all you say as my knees hit the floor in front of you.

I wrap my arm around your waist, pulling you onto my face. The palm of my hand exposes your clit, as my fingers push deeper inside of you. I take my tongue and slide it between your lips and over your throbbing clit.

You grab the back of my head and press me harder into you. "Oh god, baby, don't stop! Your tongue feels so amazing!" You say as I suck your clit into my mouth and stimulate it with my tongue. Your hips begin to writhe. I feel the rest of your body tense as you hold your breath, your hands clenching my hair tight.

You begin cuming down my fingers. You scream a broken, "Yesss-sss!"

I continue fucking you harder with my fingers, begging your body to continue coming. My tongue lightly flicks around your clit. Your body calms for a second, but I don't stop. Then you cum again for me even harder.

You gasp in pleasure as your body twitches above me. You grip my hair with a fist and pull my mouth away from you. I gently slide my fingers out of your pussy as I look up at you to see you staring down at me.

Now, it is my turn to clean my fingers with my tongue and take in the sweetness of your cum. When I finish, I just smile at you. I wrap my arms around your waist and turn my head to the side, pulling you tight against me. You rest the back of your head against the wall, and your hands relax at the back of my head. I hold you until your body's spasms cease.

I rise to stand in front of you, dragging my hands softly up your back. I pull you into me and kiss you gently. Then I exit the stall to clean my face and hands.

A moment later, you come behind me, wrap your arms around me, and kiss my neck. I look at you in the mirror and smile at you, leaning my head against yours. You smile back at me. We share a wanting gaze for a moment, then we turn and leave the bathroom.

We take our time casually walking back to the truck through the parking lot. I wear a confidant grin, watching you walk just a few steps ahead of me. You look back once, catching me watching you. You give me a pleased smile before you step to the passenger side of the truck and open the door.

I close the door for you, then I walk to the driver's side and get in. We smile at each other once again before I reach over and kiss you. As I pull away from your lips, I start the truck and slowly start to pull out of our parking spot. I take a moment for one last, long look at you before we get back on the highway.

YOUR FIRST TIME

We're at the house of my best friend, DC, and you're dressed in a low-cut black shirt and tight jeans. I'm wearing some of my nice jeans and a green, fitted shirt to bring out my eyes.

After dinner and a couple of drinks, we all gather in the living room and start singing karaoke. You and DC are battling back and forth, which is getting me all kinds of hot and bothered. (Your voice is so mesmerizing that it makes my heart pound in my chest.)

After a couple of songs, you get up to go to the bathroom. I give you a moment before I follow you. As you start to come out of the bathroom, I block your way and take you back in, shutting the door behind me with one hand. I hold your waist with my other hand. I take my hand off the door handle and slide it over your cheek to the back of your head and kiss you hard, taking your breath away. Your cheeks flush with excitement. I press your back hard against the wall, and your hands automatically swing back to grip the wall as if to catch yourself from falling. I lighten up the pressure and glide my hand around your chin, directing your head with my thumb.

I move my other hand to your ass, pulling you close as my lips make their way down the front of your neck, across your collarbone, and back up behind your ear. You start to breathe heavy as I sink my teeth into your skin. You take your hands off the wall and pull your nails across my back. I release my bite, look at you, and smile. I steal another brief kiss, and then I lead the way out of the bathroom.

We go back into the living room, and you sing a couple of songs while I melt into the couch. I become wetter and hornier with every note you sing. After a few songs and drinks, I decide it's time to show you around the house.

I tell the girls I'm going to give you the full tour, and they know that we aren't coming back. I lead you up the stairs to the attic, taking you about halfway into the room to the dividing wall. I grab your hips and put you up against the doorway that separates the two rooms.

I grab one of your hands and hold it above your head. My other hand grabs your ass and pulls your pussy onto my leg that is between yours. Your free hand is caressing the back of my head as we kiss. I slowly release your hand above your head and gently trace your face.

Once my fingers reach our lips, I pull away and begin watching where my fingers travel down to your body. I take my thumb and rub it over your slightly swollen lower lip, then I continue gliding my fingers down to your collarbone and between your breasts. My gaze follows my fingers until they stop, then I return to your lips.

I move my hand down to the bottom of your shirt, and then up under it. The feel of your soft skin sends shivers down my spine. I slide my hand to your back and unlatch your bra.

You begin grinding on my leg as I lift your shirt and start teasing your nipple with my tongue. Then I wrap my lips around it and suck on it. Your nails harshly dig into my back, showing your approval. I suck harder and flick my tongue over the tip of it.

When I let up, my hands find their way to the button on your pants to undo it. I slowly unzip them and glide my right hand down over your stomach to your throbbing, wetness.

I take my left hand past your navel to your bare breast. I kiss you before you can catch your breath as I tease your clit with my fingers.

After a few moments of intense kissing, I pull away and place my hands on your hips. Your breathing is labored and heavy. I move you over towards the bed, lying you down gently. I pull your pants off and undress myself for you.

I reach into my bag and pull out my handcuffs and blindfold. You just stare with wonder and excitement. I slowly climb on top of you and cuff your hands above your head and tell you not to move them. I take the blindfold and place it over your eyes.

I teasingly drag my lips across yours, and I let you guess at what I might do next. A moment later I give in to your luscious lips and kiss you. I drag my lips and tongue down your chin to your neck. I kiss your neck softly until I reach your ear. I drag my tongue along the line of your neck then nibble a bit, until you start to shiver from the chills going down your back.

I hold your cuffed hands firmly in my left hand to show you I'm in control. My right is lightly gliding across your naked body. I return to your lips with mine and kiss you deeply, taking your breath away. I take my teasing hand down between your breasts, over your navel, and to your throbbing clit, and I begin circular movements with my fingers.

I slide my hand off yours and bring it to rest on the mattress beside you. I glide my fingers off your clit and into your pulsating pussy. I begin to press them deeper until they can't go any further. I kiss you hard and start to flick my fingers within you.

A moment later, I release our kiss so you can catch your breath. I kiss my way down your chest. "God, you feel so good!" You say once you've catch your breath. I kiss you all over while my fingers penetrate you, twisting and turning as they push in and out of you.

I feel your body begin to squirm beneath mine. I intensify my wrist movements and begin to make you cum hard. "Oh FUCK, YES! Please don't stop! YES!" You scream out. The pressure of your orgasm tries to push my fingers out of your tight pussy.

As your orgasm ebbs, I lightly drag my fingers out of you and clean them off with my tongue. I smile while admiring the sight of you being submissive, then I apply my weight on top of you.

I kiss your neck and slide my tongue down the center of your body to your clit. I quickly place my mouth over your throbbing clit before you have time to react. Once you feel my tongue, your hands come flying over your head to mine. You pull my head harder onto your clit. I rotate my tongue around it, playing with it.

I then slide my tongue down between your lips and inside. I flick my tongue a couple times inside you, pull it out, and drag it hard back up to your clit. I begin to suck harder and harder. I soon let up and begin to lightly use my teeth. I focus on your G-spot, and just as you start squirming, I intensify my sucking pressure once again.

Your legs begin to squeeze around my head. Your hands wrap around my hair and hold me against you. I continue tasting you as you orgasm for me again.

Once your body relaxes back down on the mattress, you release my head, and I slide my naked body up yours, letting the softness of our skin affect you. Grabbing your cuffed hands in mine, I place them back over your head and kiss you deeply.

I release your wrists from the cuffs and remove your blindfold. You smile and pull me back down on top of you. My lips fall to yours and we kiss for a moment, then I whisper in your ear, "I've enjoyed the taste of you . . . now I want to fuck you!"

You just look at me with a smirk on your face. "I thought you just did," you say as I climb off you and reach back into my bag. I pull out my strap-on and put it on, then I return to the bed, placing myself between your legs. I slide the head into your wet pussy while watching your reaction. You grab my back as I thrust deep inside of you. I lean down and kiss you. Soft and slow at first, then I start fucking you harder and faster.

You dig your nails into my back hard. Pulling me in close, your nails drag their way down. The stinging sensation left behind by your nails sends my blood thundering through my body. I continue until you tell me that you want me to flip you over and fuck you from behind. I thrust once more before I stop and pull out of you. You let out a yelling moan; I smile and roll you over. You get on your knees and arms in front of me, arching your back, pressing your ass up at me. You look back at me over your shoulder and smile, knowing the impending pleasure I am about to give you.

I slide my dildo into your waiting pussy. I grab your hip with one hand and your hair with the other. I thrust my dildo in as I pull your hair. I fuck you hard and fast, then tantalizingly slow, until you begin moaning and screaming.

I don't stop. I keep going until I think you can't handle it anymore. I slide my hand down, over your hip to your engorged clit. I continue to fuck you, pleasing your throbbing clit. I apply pressure to it as I thrust harder and harder. Your breathing becomes shallow and quickens. Your moans intensify with every thrust. (Yes, cum for me, cum on me! I knew you'd like it!) I start rotating my hips with every thrust. You begin to cum all over my dildo as you moan and tremble.

You're weak at the knees, so I pull out of you as you collapse and twist onto your back. You pull me down to you. Softly, you kiss me and whisper a "Thank you" in what is left of your voice.

Then out of nowhere, you roll me on my back and straddle yourself over the top of me. I'm completely breathless. (I have no idea what to think about this. I know it is your first time, I just hope this isn't the last time.)

You start out leaning down on me, pressing your naked breasts against mine. The softness of your skin sends chills down my back. Then your lips tenderly brush against mine. I feel your emotions flow through our lips, and I know that you want to be here, in this moment, touching me.

Our lips press together so completely that I lose myself in your kiss. I feel one of your hands start moving over my hip and up my side. Once it reaches my breast, your hand cups around it and softly starts to caress it. Your hand lingers on my breast, playing with it and my nipple as you experience feeling another woman's breast for the first time.

(I have a feeling I am really going to enjoy you exploring my body!)

Your fingers find my nipple and start pinching and twisting and pulling on it, electrifying every cell in my body. Your touch alone may just send me over the edge, but I don't want to cum too early. I want to see where you go with it, see how adventurous you are willing to be.

You pull your lips away from mine, kissing me down the side of my neck. I turn my head, exposing the rest of my neck to you, showing you that I enjoy your lips on my body. You flick your tongue lightly over my skin, enticing me to cum, but I resist.

You make your way to my neglected breast and quickly find my nipple with your mouth. Your lips wrap around it and begin sucking it deeper into your mouth. Within seconds, you start using your tongue, flicking it, and circling it around my now hardened nipple. (Fuck, you are making it really hard not to cum for you! Especially after all the work up of me pleasing you.)

I think you know what your touch is doing to me. You release my nipple from between your lips and make your way down my body to my spread legs. You don't waste any time. You position yourself above my totally soaked, throbbing pussy. Before you do anything, you look up at me and smile.

You show me no fear or hesitation. All I see in your eyes are desire and wanting. My heart skips a beat as you lower your head between my legs. I almost lose it in anticipation of your tongue touching my clit.

I feel the heat escape from between your lips as you open your mouth and stick out your tongue to meet my hardened flesh. My pulse has quickened to the point that I feel like my heart is in my throat. The second your tongue touches me, every muscle in my body wants to tighten and convulse with ecstasy, but I continue to resist.

(Your tongue amazingly knows exactly what to do, I am impressed, and I am so going to cum for you. I can't take it any longer, I NEED to cum!)

The combination of your soft lips around my clit, the suction of your mouth, and the circling of your tongue is throwing me over the edge. I couldn't stop now even if I wanted to.

My whole body ceases up and releases into amazing convulsions of pure pleasure. "Fuck, yes! JUST like that! Please don't stop, PLEASE! I'm coming! Fuck, yes, I'm coming!"

You take my words to heart and don't stop; in fact, you actually know to intensify your suction and lighten the flicks of your tongue. (Holy fuck, I am so keeping you around!)

You don't stop pleasing me until I grab your head and push you back as I pull away from you. "Okay, okay. I give in. I'm sensitive. You're gonna have to play nice and give me a break." I say as I bring you up to lie next to me.

You are smiling with every movement, satisfied in your conquest. I just smile back at you, kiss you tenderly, and tell you, "I am so keeping you around." You just laugh and snuggle into me.

Rainy Day

It's been raining all day, and I remember how much you like walking in the rain, so I come over to your house and ask you out for a walk. We walk and talk for about an hour, not even feeling the rain. By the time we get back to the house, we are both soaking wet.

You walk straight to the bathroom, and I hesitate. Then I hear you turn on the water. I think about it for a moment, then I follow you. Coming up behind you, I slide my hands under your shirt, gliding them up your body, and kiss your neck. "Mmmmm, hi," you say as you lean back into me, welcoming my touch.

I slowly lift your shirt and your bra together up over your head. You lift your arms willingly, as the excitement builds your anticipation of what I might do next. I drop them at your feet, letting the heat of my hands graze against your breasts as they travel down your cool body to your wet pants. Goose bumps rise all over your body, and I feel your nipples harden under my touch.

I undo your pants as I continue kissing your neck and shoulders. Kneeling down behind you, at your feet, I pull your pants to the floor. I let my nails lightly drag over your skin, teasing you. I can already feel the heat from your arousal begin to pour off your body.

You step out of your pants and turn to face me, finding me kneeling before you. I kiss your navel and begin to run my hands over your hips and sides. Your skin is so soft and inviting. You look down at me, watching me for a moment, then you stand me up and press me against the wall. You kiss me hard, with an aggression I never saw coming. I kiss you back and allow my hands to glide down the lines of your back, up your sides, and over one of your breasts. Your nipples stay hard under my touch, begging me to touch them.

You take your hands down to the bottom of my shirt and pull it up over my head, forcing me to withdraw my hands from your body. My clothes drop to the floor as your hands firmly slip down my naked chest to the soaked band of my jeans. You kiss me as your fingers artfully unbutton them.

You move your hands between my wet jeans and my thighs, palm facing inward as if you could change direction at any time and pull your nails over my skin. (OMG, I want you soooo bad right now. Just the anticipation of your movements is making me wet!) You drag your tongue down my body as you pull my jeans down my legs, sending shivers up my spine and goose bumps over my entire body. "Oh my god, you are going to drive me insane!" I say as I step out of my jeans, and you kneel before me, kissing my navel downward.

I stand you up, wrap my arms around you tightly, kissing you. I take one hand and open the shower door. As one, we get in.

We let the heat of the water wash over us, warming us from the outside in, as our blood thunders through our bodies, and warming us from the inside out.

I pull you close and kiss you as the water finds its way between our bodies. My tongue slides between your lips effortlessly, meeting yours with a burning need. I moan with pleasure as our tongues dance around each other. I have one hand on the back of your neck, under your hair, and the other hand tracing the lines of your back down until I firmly grip your ass pulling you hard against me. Your hands are wrapped around my back, nails poised to penetrate my skin.

I lightly move my hand up and grab your hair. Gently, I pull your head back under the water, breaking our kiss. I drag my tongue down the front of your neck, kissing your collarbone, and make my way up to your shoulder. I feel you holding your breath in anticipation of what I'll do next, almost begging me to sink my teeth into your flesh.

You catch me off guard and begin dragging your nails down my back. I lift my head and arch my back. You take advantage of my position and kiss my neck down to my shoulder. You sink your teeth into my muscle. I tighten my grip on your hair, forcing you to release your grip on my skin. I begin kissing you down your cheek to your breast. I kiss and nibble at your nipple, allowing my body to slide down to my knees in front of you.

(God, you look like a goddess standing over me like this!)

My arms slide down your body and embrace you as I kiss around your navel and over your hips and inner thighs. My right hand firmly glides down the back of your one leg, then up the inside of the other, feeling every curve of your body. I stop just over the top of your clit, hovering just above it, teasing you with the heat of my fingers.

After a moment, I kiss your hip and allow my fingers to caress your clit. I tease you, so you grab my hair and make me look up at you. I stand up and kiss you, hard at first, then with the softness of a feather. The passion explodes between us as our tongues dance. My fingers stay on your clit, intensifying the pressure with every breath you take. You put your hand on mine and guide me deeper.

"Please, I need to feel you inside me!"

I begin to penetrate you, and your nails dig into my back. (God, I just can't get the angle I need to fully penetrate you. Fuck this, I want you screaming when you cum for me!)

I withdraw my fingers and turn you to the wall, kissing your neck. You throw your head back onto my shoulder and begin moaning in my ear, sending shivers down my spine and making me wetter than I could have imagined. Just before I drop to my knees behind you, the water turns cold.

I reach over and turn off the water and kiss you. Then I pull you out of the shower. I wrap a towel around you and slide it down your wet body to the floor. Kneeling in front of you, I kiss your inner thigh and pull you to the floor. I lay you on top of the towel and drag the backside of my hand down the center of your body. I watch your body's reaction to my touch.

As my hand reaches in between your legs, I lean down and kiss you. You pull me on top of you, and my fingers slide inside of your very hot, wet pussy. My fingers thrust in and out as our bodies move in rhythm.

I kiss your neck down to your breast, letting my tongue circle your nipple, then I lower my mouth over it. I begin sucking and nibbling on it, making you moan with pleasure. (God, I love it when you moan. Now, time to make you scream!) Your back starts arching, and your fingers intensify their grip on my back.

I ease up on your nipple and kiss my way down past your navel. I slide myself down between your legs and allow my tongue to slide over the top of your hardened clit.

My lips wrap around your clit and begin sucking as I start to pulsate my tongue against it. You begin to tense and spasm. "Oh god, yes, baby, YES!

Don't stop, PLEASE . . . DON'T STOP!" Your orgasm sends explosive sensations throughout your body as I intensify my fingers and lighten my tongue to make it last longer. I continue to please and taste you.

I withdraw my fingers from your tight, wet pussy. I drag my tongue between your wet lips and circle your hole, tasting every bit of you. Sliding my tongue back up to your clit, I intensify the pressure of my tongue. My hands move up and down your legs, dragging my nails roughly over your skin. I move my hands over your navel with a firm, constant pressure, sending sensations through your skin to your core. Your hands grab mine and squeeze, stopping them.

(I want more! I need to make you scream for mercy! I need to leave you breathless and exhausted.)

I take one hand from yours and bring it back in between your legs. My fingers slide easily back inside of you as my tongue works its way around your throbbing clit. You quickly grab my upper arm and the towel underneath you, bracing yourself.

"Oh god, I don't think—" is all you can let out before another wave of pleasure hits you once again.

My fingers find that sweet spot inside of you and indulge themselves. My tongue pulses on your clit, and my fingers apply pressure in a circular motion. I feel your hips begin to writhe beneath me to the rhythm of my fingers, so I quicken my movements in response, wrapping my free arm around your legs as you begin coming. I continue softly until your body goes limp and your grip on my arm relaxes. I gently slide my fingers from your twitching, now sensitive pussy and raise my head to look at you.

I make my way up your body, embracing you tightly, and kiss your neck softly. I let the weight of my body comfort you, then I kiss you. Surprisingly, you quickly turn me to my back and straddle me. I feel your wetness rubbing against the top of my mound. You grab both my wrists and pin me to the floor, breathless.

I look up at you, into your eyes, and smile. "Wow, baby! Now that you have me where you want me, what exactly are you going to do to me?" As the words flow from my mouth, my smile turns into a smirk while all the thoughts and images of what you might do to me flow through my mind.

You smirk back at me, and I can see that you are deciding what you are going to do first. "You'll see when I do them to you," you say as you lean down, pressing your wet breasts against mine. Your tongue reaches out towards my lips, parting them slightly.

I reach my tongue out to meet yours, but you pull your tongue away and lick my lips, teasing me. (Oh god, you are going to tease me till I explode. God, I could fuck you all night!)

My breathing becomes slightly labored and deep. "Please, please let me kiss you!" You just smile at my plea and move your way down my body. Your tongue flicks and drags over my skin like it is following an invisible train of something delicious.

When you get to my hips, you pause and look up at me with a mischievous smile. A split second later you dive towards my hip, digging your teeth deep into it. "Ahhh . . . " is all that comes out of my mouth as your lips softly surround your teeth with a shocking gentleness.

(Oh my god, I am going to cum the minute your tongue touches my clit! Just the heat of your body's closeness to it is making my body tense in anticipation!)

Slowly, I feel your teeth pull away from my hip, leaving your lips lingering over the now tender spot. You circle your tongue over your teeth marks, then kiss me. I let out a breath I've been holding since your teeth sank into me. You just chuckle at that as you move towards my mound.

At first, you hover over me, and I feel you let out a purposeful breath of hot air. The heat slowly falls around my clit, making my pulse quicken. You let your tongue reach out toward me. The excitement overwhelms me. I throw my head back and close my eyes.

The softness of your wet tongue pressing against my hardened clit sends me over the edge. I feel the rush of my orgasm flow through my body. I feel my heart beating in the back of my throat. (Fuck, YES, this is gonna be amazing!)

Within seconds, the sensation becomes overwhelming. You sense my body tense and wrap your lips around my clit and begin sucking it into your mouth as your tongue caresses around it. The speed of your tongue quickens as I start coming for you. "Holy shit, baby, don't stop! Yes, YES! FUCK YES!" Then my orgasm becomes too much for me, and I can't breathe anymore. I fall back to the floor limp and spasming.

You continue licking and sucking until I reach my hands down and pull you off of me. I try to bring you up to me, but you fall back, and instead of aiming for my clit, you start licking just under it down towards my hole. I don't push you away or try to pull you towards me. Instead, I relax and enjoy the feel of your tongue bathing in my cum.

A moment later, I feel you rise up off me and hear you moan with pleasure and satisfaction. You climb over the top of my body till you reach my lips. With a single soft kiss, you lay your body on top of me, wrapping your arms around my head. You nuzzle your cheek between my shoulder and my cheek, and kiss my neck.

Night One

So here I am, about to board a plane to finally come see you and go on our vacation. I have a little extra time on my hands, so we figure I can come to your house before we head out for our vacation. Waiting on this plane is going to drive me insane, though. We have been planning this vacation for so long now, I almost thought it was never gonna happen. I might be a little excited and anxious to come see you. It has been a while since we've seen each other.

So many things are going through my mind. Just the thought of the possibility of kissing you is sending shivers through my body. Four hours on a plane is almost too long. I don't know, will you want to kiss me as much as I want to kiss you?

I try to take my mind off the what ifs by reading the book I just downloaded. Unfortunately, the book isn't as stimulating as I'd hoped it would be. Maybe thinking about innocent things like kids and horses and dogs would be okay . . . yeah, right. I just end up thinking about watching you on a horse and I'm a goner. Fuck, I am gonna need a cold shower when I get there.

Alright, it is finally time to land this bird. I just need to keep my brain turned off. I walk through the terminal to the baggage claim, hoping it doesn't take too long to get my bags, I don't want you to be waiting for me for too long. But to my surprise, you are waiting for me at the carousel. When I see you, I'm pretty sure my heart stops beating. I can't even breathe. (You are fucking gorgeous!)

You just stand there by the post, smiling and chuckling at my reaction in seeing you. I finally catch my breath, and my wits return to me so I can walk over to you. I can't help it, so I just pick you up in a giant hug, holding you tight. I am this close to kissing you, but I think twice about it.

"Hey, honey, I thought I was gonna meet you outside." I say as you just look at me and smile.

"I thought it would be more fun to surprise you. That look on your face when you saw me was so worth it!" you say with a little laugh. (Fuck, I just want to kiss that smile off your face!) We'll just have to see what happens when I get you alone.

Finally, here comes my bag. I quickly walk over to the carousel and snatch it up over my shoulder and turn to you. You are just standing there watching me. I wander what you are thinking about. Are you as nervous as I am? Are you gonna be the aggressor, or am I?

"Okay, darlin, follow me so we can get the heck out of here."

"Yes, ma'am. I'd follow you anywhere!" I say as my eyes fall to your nice firm ass as you lead the way. (I am in so much trouble!)

Right off the bat, I know which vehicle is yours. You just walk to the back of it and open it for me. I throw my bag in the back like a sack of potatoes and close it. You lead the way to my door and open it for me. Okay, I am definitely not used to someone opening my door for me. You are cute doing it though, so I don't mind. Then you walk around the front to your door. You get in and smile at me. I can't help but smile back at you. I think about kissing you again, then you start the truck and I back down.

As we are driving back to your house, I slide a bit closer to you and lean my hand on the center console, just to feel things out. You just give me a smirk and reach down and grab my hand. The touch of your hand sends shock waves through my whole body, and I know that on the first chance I get, I NEED to kiss you!

Lucky for me, the chance comes not too long after the thought crosses my mind. You must have been thinking something along the same lines, because for some reason, you pull off the highway and into a convenient store parking lot. The second you park the truck, I automatically move towards you. I brace myself with my left hand on your console and take my right hand over your cheek as you turn to look at me. I pause for a split second to look into your eyes, then at your lips, letting you know I am going to kiss you.

I hear your breathing catch as I lean in and softly press my lips to yours. The softness is quickly replaced with the pent-up passion and desire that has been building between us. There is a hunger between us that I can feel down in my bones. Man, I am not gonna be able to restrain myself for too long! The feel of your tongue dancing with mine is sending heat throughout my entire body. (Get a grip. Breathe! You are acting like this is your first time.)

I slowly pull away from you, slowing our kiss to a teasing nibble. I open my eyes to meet yours. "God, I have wanted to do that since the day I met you! I guess it is true what they say, 'the best things in life are worth the wait.' Did you actually stop here to get something from the store or from me?"

You just laugh, then say, "Both." Then you reach behind you and open the door and proceed to get out. I just let out a deep breath and follow you. "So what do we need to get in here?"

"Beer and something to eat. You have got to be hungry after your flight, and you know I don't cook."

"Beer sounds good, but I'm actually not that hungry . . . at least for food."

"Mmmm, well, to be on the safe side, we'll get you something to keep your energy up then."

I just laugh and follow you in. You grab some beer, and I split off from you to grab some snacks. We meet up at the counter, and I beat you to the punch with the money to pay for everything. Then we head back to the truck and toss the snacks and beer in the back seats. You start the truck so fast like you needed to get us out of the parking lot before I kiss you again. I just internally laugh.

As it turns out, you actually don't live far from the Quickie Mart we were just at. That totally works for me. Since it is kinda late, I don't expect anything except, "Here is a place to sleep, and I'll see ya in the morning."

Since it is a Friday, and apparently, you have done some planning of your own, the house is empty. It is not quite what I expected, but I should know better than to expect anything. So when we pull up, everything is quiet. You grab the stuff from the back seat while I grab my bag from the back. Then I follow you in. I drop my bag by the kitchen table and take a quick look around. "Where is everyone? I figured there would be at least a boy or a dog running around."

"Dogs are outside in their house, and the boys are out for the night." As you are talking and putting stuff in the fridge and on the counters, you don't notice me coming up behind you. You finish talking and turn around just in time for me to embrace your face with my hands and steal your breath with my kiss. You brace yourself on the counter behind you as I press my body against yours. With firm pressure, I take a hand behind your ear and to the base of your neck. My other hand is busy finding its way down your body to your hip.

You take your hands off the counter and wrap them around my back. The pressure of your embrace just makes me want to touch you more! (Should I let you take the lead, or should I? Oh, why am I even contemplating this. Whatever is gonna happen is gonna happen. If you want to take the lead, you will, and I won't stop you! If not, I surely don't mind. Lord knows I have all kinds of ideas on what to do with you.)

As my mind races, your body answers all my questions. Your hands make their way to my ass and mine find a way to tangle themselves in your clothes. One hand is occupied with removing your shirt while the other one is gliding up to your breast. The moment my hand slides under your bra to touch your soft nipple, your hands go to the hem of your shirt to assist me in ripping it off of you, which, unfortunately, required us to stop kissing. The hidden blessing in that is that it gives me a chance to take you in. (Yeah, there is no way in hell I am gonna be able to keep my hands to myself!)

"You are beautiful!" I say as I look you up and down, stopping on your lips, breasts, and hips. You just watch me breathlessly, waiting to see what I will do or say. Until I take a little too long, you just decide that you need to take your bra off for me. I still can't bring myself to move, so you place a hand under my chin, bringing my eyes to meet yours. Then you slowly lean in to kiss me while continuing our eye contact. From there on, I have absolutely no question in my mind that WE wanted this.

My grip on your breast increases as I work my fingers around your nipple while my lips make their way to your neck. I want to ravage you, but at the same time, I want to savor every inch of your body. But yeah, ravaging wins. I sink my teeth into your shoulder at the bottom of your neck while I pull your hips hard against me. You stop your hands in the middle of my back and dig your nails in, which I know took a lot because you don't have nails. "Uhhhhh!" is all you let out. The best part is it is right in my ear. (Fuck, I am wet!)

I release my teeth and let my lips linger over the marks I have left. My tongue plays while my lips caress your soft skin. You slowly release your grip, then I let your hands work their way up my back to remove my bra. I pause what I am doing to allow you to remove it, but mainly so I can make sure your hands are busy while I make my way down to your pants.

In the time it takes you to toss my bra to the kitchen floor, my hands feel your waistband to undo your button and zipper, and I am already halfway to my knees pulling your pants off when your hands land on my shoulders, causing me to freeze. I land on one knee and look up at you. You just look at me with that "What the hell have I gotten myself into?" look. It takes only a moment before I answer your look with a response.

In response, as I maintain eye contact with you, I press my hands to the floor with your jeans and boots. You kindly assist me in my actions while I take my upright knee and leaned in to the right, forcing you to spread your legs as you shift your weight to stay balanced. I slowly lean into your thigh and start kissing you as I begin to trace your calves with my hands. I watch you shiver under my touch.

You take your hands through my hair to the back of my neck. (Oh fuck. She is gonna turn me into putty if she keeps that up.) I quickly react by kissing you up your inner thigh. It works, since your hands pause on the back of my neck. Then to my amusement, you direct my head between your legs. I sure as hell am not gonna fight you on this one—except to tease you. I hover over your clit and take deep, heavy breaths, allowing the heat of my breath to wash over your clit.

"Oh god, please. Please just touch me, taste me. I'm gonna fucking go insane if you don't make me cum soon!" And on that note, I go all in. The look on your face tells me all I need to know. I wrap my lips around your throbbing clit. The heat coming off you is intense, I don't know how long you are gonna be able to last.

Your hand resting on the back of my head starts to apply a constant pressure, and the other one starts to curl around the edge of the counter's edge. That's it—now time to send you over the edge. I twirl my tongue around your clit as I begin sucking you into my mouth. I know you can only take so much of the intense suction, so I switch it up on you just as I feel your body starting to tense. I flatten my tongue over your clit and proceed to move in slow, very firm circles. (Yup, that did it.) You start coming so hard I feel it begin to cover my chin. (Oh hell, no, this is not going to waste!) I lighten my tongue over your clit and move to your opening so I can better taste you.

Your body is spasming and tensing over me. I can't help but want to continue touching you, so I quickly stand up, grab you by the hips, and take you over to the table. "Oh god, what are you doing to me! Don't stop, please don't stop!" you say breathlessly.

"Don't you worry, honey, I'm just getting started," I say as I lay you on the table.

"What do you—" is all you can let out before I slide my fingers between your legs. You're more than ready for me to penetrate you. "Hmmm, I could stay inside you forever. You feel so good!"

I work my fingers in and out in a steady motion at first. Now I want to see how much you want me, so I intensify my movements and add some finger thrumming on the backside of your clit. You claw at me to bring me over the top of you. My fingers work inside of you as I kiss you with reckless abandon. I can't get enough of you! And from the way your hands are moving over my body, I know you want me.

"I need to feel you cum for me again. Cum for me." And to assist you with that request, I become more aggressive with my fingers. I watch your reaction as I kiss my way over your collarbone down to your breast and circle your nipple with my tongue.

"Uhhhhh, hmmm! Why do you have to torture me?" I know what you are referring to. So on that note, I engulf your nipple with my mouth. As I suck, I feel your body tense and start spasming beneath me. "Oh FUCK, FUCK!" Then all the breath in you leaves your body with a spasm. I want to take you over the edge, so I am not about to let up. I want to see how much you can take. I suck hard on your nipple right before I start to bite down, just hard enough to make you scream with pleasure, not pain.

Before I know it, you have your hand in my hair. Your grip is intense. I know it is time to let up; I don't want to yet, but I do. I release your nipple and lighten up with my fingers. "Ah, not yet. Don't pull out yet." Curious . . . not that I want to pull out, anyways. I change up my finger movements, and the look on your face goes from "I need to take it slow and prepare to withdraw" to "Holy fuck, don't even think about stopping!" And well, since I am thoroughly enjoying pleasuring you, I am not about to disappoint you.

I keep eye contact with you while I kiss my way down your body. You watch me with a sense of anticipation and intense desire. (I could swim in those eyes!) "What do you want me to do to you?"

"I want you to continue to fuck me until I can't take it anymore!"

"And how will I know when you can't take it anymore?"

"I will stop you!"

"Hmmm, so then how would you like me to fuck you until then?"

"Any way you want . . . just don't stop what you're currently doing!"

"Yes, ma'am!" I say with a curt nod, then I proceed to burry my face between your legs on top of your clit. Between my fingers and mouth, this shouldn't take long. Your hands caress the top of my shoulders and the back of my head. (You are gonna make me cum just by playing with my head!) This won't do; I need to get you off so I can turn you over!

"Oh fuck, I'm gonna cum . . . don't stop, please don't stop!" you say as if on cue. (And within a few seconds of your body calming down, I am gonna have you bent over this table.)

Little do I know what is going through your head. You sit up and grip my hair, pulling me away from you. I take the hint and slowly remove my fingers from your body. But I also can't waste a good desert, so while I am looking at you, I bring my fingers to my mouth and clean them off slowly while you watch me. I can hear that you are holding your breath while my tongue works its way around and between my fingers.

Within seconds, you are off the table and have me pinned on the floor. My hands are pinned above my head while you straddle me. "Done?" I say with a big "job well done" grin.

"For now. I can't take it anymore. I need to taste you!" And with that statement, you glide your hands down my body to the button of my jeans beneath your body, then you stop and look up at me, questioning.

"What's wrong?"

"Nothing just deciding what I want to do to you."

"Oh, is that all? I have a few ideas if you need any. " I don't think you do; I think you know exactly what you want to do to me. And within a matter of two seconds, you kneel next to me, taking my jeans and underwear off in one fell swoop, leaving barely enough time for me to kick off my shoes before you get to my ankles. I'm excited to see what you have come up with. Lord knows, I am beyond ready to cum. Watching you get off makes me so freaking wet!

What are you doing? You look and then turn away from me, then you turn back to watch my reaction. You straddle my face, facing toward my body. (Holy fuck, yes!) Then you "walk" your way down my body on your hands so that you are lying on top of me. (Oh, now I am in heaven. This is gonna be fun!) I think, just in time for you to wrap your arms around my thighs and place your lips ever so hungrily over my clit. I bury my face between your legs and absolutely gorge myself. I start with teasing your hole, then I make my way to your clit. (Fuck, I can't focus, I can't even think clearly!)

Your tongue is dancing over my clit while you run your hands over my thighs and moan into me. (I am so gonna cum if you keep this up!) I can't contain myself anymore, I moan over your clit as I press my fingers deep into you. I need you to cum with me.

Your reaction to my fingers is to intensify the movements of your tongue and to slide your fingers deep inside me. I didn't expect that. (Holy shit, I am so not gonna make it!) I can't help it; I release your clit and begin to arch myself into you. I need more; I want more. I can't get enough of the way you are making me feel. "Oh god, please don't stop, honey. I'm so close. Fuck, you feel so good!"

At the same time, I feel your body tensing with my fingers still penetrating you. (Fuck yeah, cum with me! This may send me over the edge.) Just thinking about it, I intensify my finger movements, and with my intensity comes yours. (This is freaking HOT!) Within moments, we both begin coming. I relent first, removing my fingers from inside of you so I can grip you as long as I can stand it. I place both hands on your sides, then your hips, and then, because I can't take the intensity I am feeling, I grab at the floor, then place one hand in your hair and one in mine.

"Fuck, I can't. I can't take it anymore." I try to pull you to me, but you are voracious. The moans coming from you as you devour me is so fucking stimulating. (I am so gonna lose this battle. How much can I really take?) Then you do something with your tongue that shoots an intense heat throughout my entire body. (Yes, I need more of that. More, I just need more) "God, yes, forget what I just said, don't stop! Whatever you are doing, just don't stop! Mmmmmmm . . . please!"

I don't want to touch you right now for fear it will either change my awareness of the strokes of your tongue or change the intensity of the movement of your fingers. (I need to do something with my hands.) Just as the thought comes to me, you pause what you are doing to readjust your position. You position yourself so that you are between my legs looking up at me. (I am in so much trouble!)

You purposely keep your eyes glued to mine as you slowly lean in and reach your tongue out to meet my pulsing clit. "God, that is sexy!" is all I can say as your tongue becomes enraptured with my clit. You of course don't stop there; you place one hand on my hip tattoo and trace it with a strange intensity that actually arouse me further, and the other one on my inner thigh, teasing me with your fingers.

I arch my hips into you, so your tongue's pressure intensifies just enough to send me over the edge. I buck wildly under your touch with the waves of electricity pulsing through me. You lighten your touch and ever so slowly lighten your suction on my clit, not by much though, because you want me to ride out the orgasm for as long as possible while you take your time enjoying the process of licking all the cum off me.

I can't talk, all I am able to do is think and shiver. My throat feels like someone stole my voice box; my whole neck is numb, along with my hands and feet. (Good lord, when I get the feeling back in my extremities, you are in so much trouble!) Like you can tell that I am thinking all kinds of thoughts, you crawl over the top of me, lie directly on top of me. The pressure of your body feels amazing! Then you kiss me, soft and gentle as if you know I can't handle intense touching in that moment. Then you whisper, "And this is only night one." I just smile and close my eyes.

A Day for Riding

As I start to wake up, I can sense you moving around me. I don't open my eyes readily; I want to try and figure out what you are up to first. From what I can tell, you are getting dressed and highly energized. Just out of curiosity, I slowly open my eyes. Inwardly, I am hoping you aren't looking at me so I can watch you for a moment. To my surprise, you are bending over to pull on your boots. (Totally an image I will enjoy remembering.) I have to keep reminding myself that I can't just grab you and pull you onto the bed with me, which is like convincing a child that they don't want ice cream.

You must have sensed me watching you because you turn your head in my direction and look over your shoulder to meet my gaze. I give you the "cat caught drooling over the bird in a cage" look, and you just laugh. You slowly straighten your body, rolling your hips, of course. (God, you have to know how much that makes my pulse race!)

"Good morning, Sweetie," you say as you turn to me and make your way to the bed.

I sit up lazily, thinking about how much I want you naked and crawling your way over me. (I am in so much trouble!) "Good morning, Sunshine! How long have you been up?"

"Not too long."

"And what has you so energized? Wanna share some of that energy?"

You just give me a look like you have been starving for weeks and I am a nice juicy stake that has been put on a silver platter in front of you. And just as I am going to say something, you read my mind and put a knee on the bed next to me. You may not be naked, but that can quickly change.

You straddle me like I am your horse. Slowly, you lean over me, pressing your hips down over mine, and forcing yourself hard against me. You lean down, toss your hair to one side, and hover over my lips. Your eyes never leave mine. We don't talk, and we just sit there like that for a moment. Then you lean in and graze my lips with yours and flex your hips forward. I don't know how much more I can take before I grab and roll you over.

Just when I think I may burst, you kiss me hard, taking my breath. Our tongues intertwine like a rope that has been braided for years. I take a hand down the small of your back, finding that little opening between your jeans and your ass. My other hand glides up the back of your neck and tangles in your hair. After last night, you don't realize the monster you've awakened.

Thankfully, you aren't wearing paint-on jeans. My hand slides successfully to your ass cheek, which I firmly grip and forcefully pull hard against me. (I need to have you.) I can't take much more; just the feel of you makes me wet. Then out of nowhere, you take your arms under each of my shoulders and flip us.

After I catch my breath, I thrust my hips into you. You moan against my mouth, causing shivers to shoot down my back. Now my hunger shows. I become relentless in my pursuit to rid you of what little clothing you are able to put on before I wake up. My lips chase my hands down your body. I don't even take the time to fully take your clothes off. I don't have the patience to unbutton each button of your shirt, so I just rip it open. I can hear the buttons hitting the wood flooring, and 'm pretty sure I owe you a new one now. The white "wife beater" underneath is loose enough that I am able to take a single hand, lift it up over your head, and leave it on the back of your neck. Lucky for me, it is a day you decided not to wear a bra.

My mouth hungrily finds your nipple quickly. I try to somewhat restrain myself, but I can't. You taste so damn good. It is like the taste of you is the water I have been searching for in the desert for days.

Your moans are coming quicker and are becoming hoarser. You take a hand to the back of my head, rubbing your fingers firmly over every single nerve. I suck your nipple into my mouth hard, then I let my teeth tell you how hungry I am for you. You buck your hips into my grinding hips. (It is a damn good thing I haven't changed yet; otherwise, I'd be walking around with wet underwear all day!)

As you buck against me, I slowly release your nipple from between my lips, being reminded of what I really want with every buck of your hips. Before I completely move on, I allow my tongue to twirl around your nipple as I exhale the heat from my mouth over it. "Fuck me . . . or are you going to tease me all morning?" is all you are able to let out.

I just look up at you and smile. Just because I know you want it so bad, now, I have to take my time, at least, for a little bit. I slowly drag my tongue in a crisscross motion down your abs, over to your sides and back. I feel your eyes following me, your gaze burning into my head like hot lasers. I will not look you in the eyes, though. I have things to do to you that take strength and focus.

You continue to buck and twist under me, and I move over you. I can feel your frustration and invigoration in your movements. You can't keep still, and you grip and re-grip at the bedding beneath you. It takes everything I have not to smile at that. I need you frustrated and hungry. I methodically unbutton your jeans, hooking a single finger on the corner of your jeans at your hip and pull them down just a little bit. Just enough to expose your hip enough for me to kiss.

And just as I think you can't take it anymore, I take my other hand in your waist band, rear up on my knees, and pull your jeans down to the top of your boots. I pull you to the edge of the bed by hooking my hands behind your knees. You pull yourself up into a sitting position on the edge of the bed, with your hands pressed hard into the mattress behind you. I finally look you in the eyes and smile as I lean into kiss your mound.

You just watch me move in on you, until my tongue connects with your clit. I keep my eyes locked with yours. I want to see your reaction. My tongue flattens over your clit as I slide my body slightly towards the floor. Your body moves to meet my tongue, eager to be tasted, eager to be devoured. Your clit reaches the back of my throat, and the tip of my tongue curls to enter you. I want all of you—to taste you, to please you.

The moment my tongue slides into you, our little game of who will blink first ends. You throw back your head and let out a moan that sends goose bumps all over every inch of my skin once again. I close my eyes and think of all the things I want to do to you. I organize my thoughts while my tongue works in circles. (Yes, that's it. I know exactly what I need to do.)

I open my eyes just enough to move my hands into position, then I close them again, taking the scent of you in. I slowly drag my tongue from inside you and flick it past the side of your clit. I notice a change in your body and a silence, so I look up. I find you looking down at me. "Why did you stop?" you ask with this pouty face and shimmering eyes. I don't stop to answer you with my words; I just smile with my eyes and thrust my fingers deep inside you.

I do not move them once they are stopped by your body. I wait for you to slightly relax, then I begin vibrating them within you. My tongue creates a slight suction with my lips around your clit. Then I wait for you to fully react. It doesn't take long. I feel your body heating up. Your breathing is deepening, and I can see your eyes starting to get heavy as your head rolls to the side.

I know it is time. Enough teasing. I work my fingers to the backside of your clit and begin massaging the area. The combination is making you weak. I notice your arms are sliding outwards as your eyes close. I watch you lick your lips. (That does it—no more waiting.)

Just as I feel your body tense, I stop sucking your clit and pull myself up on my left arm over the top of you, and as my tongue reaches for your nipple, I begin thrusting hard with my fingers. In a matter of moments, you cum around my fingers, spasming so hard I almost can't keep you on the bed with my body.

"AHHHH . . . FUCK YES! Don't fucking stop. Just don't stop!" (Your wish is my command!) I don't stop. I fuck you with my fingers until you can't orgasm anymore. I release your nipple and work my way up to your neck, kissing my way to your ear. "Thanks for sharing. I knew you'd help me get energized," I whisper.

Then I pull my finger out of you, kiss you on the lips, and push myself off the bed into a standing position. With a smug, satisfied look on my face, I look you at you from boots and jeans to torn button-up and tank top. You just look at me in bewilderment as I turn and walk to the bathroom in my boxers.

(Goddamn, I am so wet! I can wait though. I want to see what you have planned for the rest of the day. And now that I am energized, I am ready for the day.)

I manage to turn the shower on and strip off my boxers by the time you manage to clean yourself up, pull up your pants, and right your shirt. As I start to climb into the shower, I feel you looking at me again. I turn to see you leaning against the doorjamb. The shine in your eyes is enough to stop anyone in their tracks. You look amazing with your "I just had my brains fucked out of me" look. The disheveled hair and buttonless shirt do so many things to me.

"What was that?"

"I asked if you wanted to share some of that energy with me, and you came over to me with that look in your eyes, so I took advantage of you. Did you not want me to?"

"Now, I'm not saying that at all. I was just wondering where that came from."

"Ah well, I had an amazing night, woke up drained and horny, and well, you looking the way you do, I knew the best way to get me energized would be to taste you. The minute the thought even crossed my mind, there was nothing I could do to stop it. I do apologize for the shirt though. I will get you another one if you like."

You just chuckle and then approach me slowly. "I don't care about the shirt. That was HOT as all hell! I just wasn't expecting you to get energized so quickly. It caught me off guard."

"That was the plan. I find that the best things happen when you aren't expecting it. Kinda like last night. Or did you expect that to happen?"

"Umm, hoped would be more accurate description of my feelings about what happened last night. I, however, didn't have any expectations or know how hot it would be."

"Well, that is news to me. You play things close to the vest, so I just figured I'd take a shot in the dark, and if it worked out, well, I had plenty of ideas of what I wanted to do to you and with you."

"I have an idea or two as well. So hurry up in there and get dressed. We have places to be and things to do today." Then you lean in past the shower curtain, look me up and down, smile, and then kiss me. You back away slowly, then turn on your heels and look over your shoulder at me as you leave the room. I, of course, can't help but watch you walk away.

I take what has got to be the quickest shower ever, jump out, and almost forget to towel off before walking into the room to get dressed. I just walk into your room with a towel kinda wrapped around me and head towards my bag. I don't see you when I get in there, but I think I hear you in the kitchen. I drop my towel and start digging into my bag for something to wear for the day. But I have no clue what we are doing for the day, so I just think of what you are wearing and pull out clothes accordingly.

I lay my clothes on the bed and begin to bend down to put on my boxers; however, it seems you have a different plan, since you, at that moment, step behind me and on my boxers. At the same time, you wrap your arms around me. "My turn."

Within moments of your touching me, my body is begging for you. I stand up as I release my underwear and let them drop to the floor. I reach my hands back to your thighs and pull you closer. I look over my shoulder at you. You bring a hand up my navel, past my breasts to my neck. You hold me in that position and kiss me hungrily. Your other hand reaches between my legs and easily glides a couple of fingers past my lips to my already throbbing clit.

Because you are a little taller than I am, this position is actually quite comfortable and well, HOT. You press hard against my clit, forcing me to press my bare ass hard against you. My hips go on automatic. I start grinding against you as your fingers work me over. Your lips slowly caress mine as our tongues dance around each other.

I don't know how much I can take. Lord knows how ready I am when I walk away from you. Then, without warning, you spin me around and drop to your knees. I look down at you as you are reaching between my legs. I think you are going to touch me again, but I am wrong. You hook my leg and place it over your shoulder as you lean into me. I almost lose my balance, but then I reach down and place my hands on your head and shoulder. You just look up at me and grin as you lean in between my thighs.

(Oh god, your tongue . . . I am never going to last!) I think, as I let out a pleased moan.

You start out slow and methodical, licking around my clit, then over it. You flatten your tongue, then soften it ever so slowly. Your breath lingers on every part of my mound. Heat waves are shooting through my body. I know without a doubt I will be coming for you very soon. Which ends up being sooner than I think.

Once again without warning, you lift me up by slightly standing up, which puts me on my back on the bed. Your lips don't leave me for long. And with the return of your lips and tongue, you take a hand over my ass cheek to my pussy. You twist your fingers inside of me and curl them. Your tongue circles my clit while your lips begin sucking. (Holy shit, I am gonna lose it!)

Before I even know I am cuming, I begin spasming and clench around your fingers inside of me. "Oh fuck, yes! Yessss . . . " You lighten up the pressure of your tongue and your suction to keep my orgasm going as long as I can stand it. I try to endure it for as long as possible, but I can't take it for too long. I place a hand on your head, then move your long hair out of my way so I can look at you. You look up at me and withdraw your fingers in a slow, drawn out movement. You begin to smile at me, first with your eyes, then with your mouth, relinquishing the hold you have over my clit.

I just fall to the bed twitching. You laugh as you crawl over the top of me and make me look at you. "Now that is better. Come on, get dressed lazy butt. We have things to do today." Then you lean down and kiss me. (Fucking hell . . . she has no idea what she is doing to me! Well, she might.)

You leave the room, looking back at me like I did to you, leaving me to be the one to clean myself up and get dressed. I lie there on the bed for a moment, gathering myself. Then I reach for the towel I had just been using and clean myself up. I quickly dress, still very curious as to what we are actually going to be doing for the day.

****

"So what is it that you have planned for our day, anyways? What's the rush?" I say as I approach you in the kitchen.

"We are going riding. I'm gonna introduce you to my horses, and I figured I could take you on one of the trails I like riding."

"Ah, now it all makes sense. Well, I'm ready. Are you?"

"Let me just find where I threw my key last night, and we can head out."

Knowing how special this day actually is to you, I reach over the dining room table and retrieve the keys for you. Although I do enjoy watching you bend over every five seconds, I think it will be more beneficial to get us on the road as soon as possible.

"Found 'em," I say as I hold them up for you to see. I just smile at you and grab my coat. You snatch the keys from me with a kiss, and we are off.

We pull into the ranch about twenty-five minutes later. I watch you become more excited the closer we get. It just makes me smile. Then I look over to the pasture to our right, and I see all the horses out grazing and playing. Man, what a beautiful sight! "They are beautiful! Where are your boys?"

"They are in their stalls. They knew I was coming in today."

"Huh, now look who is full of surprises." I say with a smart-ass grin.

You park the truck and we get out. You walk around the front and make a beeline to the barn, then you pause at the door and turn back to me to see if I am coming. "Don't worry about me, honey, I'm right behind you. I like the view better from this angle. But seriously, I'm right behind you, lead the way." So you turn around and lead the way.

It is like the horses know you are coming. You don't even have to say anything; they just smell you or sense you coming, and they both stick their heads out over their stall doors and look towards you. The minute you see them, your stride lengthens and speeds up a little. It is very endearing. As you approach them, you call out their names, and they talk back to you. I can tell they are happy to see you too.

You stop at the first stall and make introductions, and I slowly raise my flat palm to him and let him smell me. Once I know he is okay with me, I start petting him and talking to him. Then you turn to the next stall and we repeat the process.

"So now that I have met these magnificent boys, which one am I riding, and where is their gear?"

"You'll be riding this one, the one I am currently petting. And as for their gear, it is hanging up on the wall across from their stalls. Do you want me to show you how to put it on him?"

"I think I still remember how. It has been a while, but if I need an assistance, I'll call you over. The quicker we get them saddled, the quicker you can show me the trail you enjoy so much."

"Yes, ma'am! I will leave you two to it then." You just walk over to the wall behind us and grab a bit, then walk towards the other stall. I just follow suit. When I get back to my horse, I start up a conversation with him. As he talks back to me, I slip his bit in and wrap the harness over his ears, then I pull him out of the stall to the walk way, tie him to his door, and start bringing his blanket and saddle over. By the time I finish buckling him up, you walk over and check my work to make sure it is tight enough. I don't mind; I would rather you check them than fall off. You just look at me like "Wow, you do know what you are doing." Then you walk to grab your horse, and we walk them out of the stables.

As we exit, the owner comes over and introduces herself. It is a short introduction, then we mount the horses and walk them down the road a bit past the pastures. "So what are you comfortable doing on a horse?"

"Not running."

You just laugh at me. "Okay, how about a gallop?"

"Sounds good. I'll follow you."

"Of course, you will," you say as you take off with a smile.

I just laugh and put my heels into the sides of my horse. You lead us into a nicely wooded area that has a well-ridden path. About five minutes into the ride, I start to hear water running. You slow your horse to a walk so I can catch up to you.

As I approach you, I slow my horse to ride alongside you. "So how do you like the ride so far?"

"I'm loving it! He has a smooth stride. And the scenery is gorgeous. I can see why you enjoy it so much. It is very serene and peaceful."

"I thought you'd enjoy it. Just wait, you haven't seen the best part yet."

"I can't wait."

Then we just ride in silence, listening to the scenes unfold around us. We climb a slight embankment then head towards a ridge, where the forest opens up into a plateau of wild flowers and wheat grass. (Man, if I ever needed to find peace, this is where I would find it!)

Lost in the scene around me, I don't notice you veering off to the right until I hear you yell for me. I just smile at you as I snap out of my zone. I dig my heels in to catch up to you, then I slow down again. We are headed towards a downed tree by a ridge.

You pull up next to the tree and dismount your horse, so I do the same. We tie our horses up to a branch that rises about four feet off the trunk. Then you walk me over to the other side of the tree so I can fully see the view before us.

It is a bunch of ridge lines full of trees and wheat grass with blue skies and painted on version of clouds. Seriously it looks like a painting. As we turn back towards the tree and horses, I can see that you and probably many others have spent some time up here because all the grass around the tree area is matted flat.

You walk to your horse, but I just stop by the tree. I don't want to go yet. Then you turn to me and smile. "Don't worry, we aren't leaving yet. I figured we could have lunch here."

"Great thinking! What can I do to help?"

"Can you grab the blanket out of the other side pouch?"

"On it. Anything else?"

"Nope, got everything else already."

I walk over towards to edge, then I lay out the blanket. You join me, placing the bundle of food in the middle of the blanket. Lucky for us there isn't too much of a wind today, just a slight breeze. I watch you unwrap the towel with some bread and cheese in it. Then you get up and go back to the side pouch. You pull out a couple of waters and return to the blanket with them. As you sit down next to me, you hand me one of them.

I crack it open and take a large drink. Then I look over at you and find you watching me. "What?"

"Nothin'. Just enjoying the view." At that, I just smile and lean over to kiss you.

"Thank you!" I say as your lips part. I'm not quite sure what I'm expecting, but the next thing I know, I am on my back and you are straddling me again. You pin my arms above my head and just look down at me like you are deciding what you want to do with me. Your hair gently tickles the side of my face while you decide.

The vision of you with your arms above your head, your hair tossed to one side, blocking the sun, and the blue skies behind you is simply breathtaking. I am in absolutely no rush to change the scene unfolding before me. Then something shifts in your eyes. They light up with knowing. You have decided what is coming next for me.

As you lean down and kiss me gently, you take a hand to your jeans. I don't question what you are up to; I just want to enjoy you. I take my free hand to the back of your head behind your ear and caress you. It doesn't take you long to finish what you are doing and bring your hand over the top of mine.

You take my hand from your head and guide it between our bodies. You flatten my palm against your stomach and press it past your jeans, over your very wet mound. I take your guidance and press farther until the palm of my hand is over your clit and my fingers are perched at your opening, just waiting for a signal from you that this is what you want.

I don't have to wait long. You thrust your hips forward and down hard onto me. The back of my palm is pressed hard against my clit. With every thrust, you not only force me inside you but also create a friction against me. (This is perfect!)

You continue kissing me, teasing me with your tongue. My pulse is racing, and I'm pretty sure I am not breathing for myself. You take your free hand off my arm and place it next to my ear. Your hand curls over the top of my head and starts clawing at my nerves. I know you are getting excited. The way your hips begin to move makes it impossible for anyone to do anything else but get excited.

Then to slightly throw you off and extend this experience, I start rolling my hips in a circular motion side to side. You take that moment to show off your riding skills and start riding me like I am a house galloping.

(Oh fuck, I am gonna lose it before I even have a chance to catch my breath!)

Just as the thought enters my mind, I sense your breathing change, and before I can react, you start cuming for me. Your spasms force the back of my hand hard against my pulsating clit. It isn't but a moment before I am coming with you. You hold my head tight against you, which just turned our kiss into a hungry tornado of tangling movements.

The rawness of your movements over me gives me that little extra bit I need not to buck you off me and take in the pleasure. Lucky for me, you slow your movements into a seductive roll after a few minutes. My hips are reduced to sporadic spasms under you.

You take your hand from the top of my head and grip my chin, instantly stopping me from kissing you. You tease my lips with your tongue. Then you turn my head to one side and lick from my jawline to my ear. You bite my earlobe hard then slowly pull away enough to release it. "Now that is how I like to go riding."

(God, you are so HOT right now!) I pull my hand quickly from your jeans to the back of your head, grab a chunk of hair tight against your scalp, and forcefully roll us. I pin your hands to the blanket and kiss you hard.

Vacation

Armed with only a to-go bag and a condo reservation, we land and head straight for the rental cars. I made all the reservations, so you don't have to worry about anything. Luckily, they are ready for our arrival, so it doesn't take long.

Once they hand me the keys, we are off. The car isn't too far from the door, so I hit the trunk button for the car. You and your long legs get to the car before I do; I don't mind, though, I like the view. You carefully place your bag in the trunk then reach for mine as I approach. You just toss it next to yours, and I shut the trunk door. We both make a beeline to our doors, get in, and just sink into our seats for a moment.

After we catch our breath, I start the car and program the address of the condo into the car's navigation system. You just sit there watching me. I take a moment to look at you from the console. You are just watching me with wander. You hate electronics, or they hate you. Either way, I will be the one navigating this trip. I just want to give you a few days where you don't have to worry or think about anything.

I can't decide if I should just give you the "I got this" smile or lean over and kiss you. I think I'll wait to kiss you. You look like you are ready for a little down time, so I just give you a smile and then put the car in gear. Plus, the condo isn't far from the airport; it is only about fifteen minutes.

You just lean back in your seat and melt into it. I do what I can to focus on the road and the turns. Luckily, the navigation system tells me where I need to turn. Right now, with you all relaxed and your eyelids falling, I just want to watch you.

I reach over and lace my arm over the backrest and allow my hand to drape over your seat to your head. I lightly move the hair covering your face and put them behind your ear. Gently, I play with your hair, showing you that it is okay for you to close your eyes. You let out a soft moan and let me continue to rub your head at least until I pull into the driveway of our condo building.

I run my hand down the side of your cheek to let you know we have arrived. You lazily open your eyes and just look at me. I laugh and get out of the car to check us in.

By the time I return to the car, you are standing outside of it, waking up and getting ready to pop the trunk. I, however, stop you. "No need, honey. Our condo is in the back by the water, and our parking spot is just outside of it."

"Nice! How did you swing that?"

"I got connections," I say as I start smiling and opening your door for you. You give me a look then fall into the seat. I quickly close the door and walk to my side and get in. I pull the car around the main building to a parking lot lined with bungalows. I pull into the third parking spot in front of the second bungalow.

"Wow, this is where we are staying?"

"Yup!" I say as I put the car in park and open my door. You sit there looking at it for a second, then you get out to join me at the trunk. I have already grabbed both our bags and am in the process of closing the trunk when I see you. You look like you want to say something, but you decide against it.

We walk to the door and I have you fetch the keys out of my front pocket. "Now, aren't you glad I didn't wear my tight jeans today?" You just look up at me and smile as you struggle to get the key. When you finally manage, you smile and just turn to unlock the door.

When you open the door, you push it open for me and let me walk through first. You follow after me, shutting the door behind us. I walk past the back of the couch down the hallway to the first open door I find and drop our bags on the bed. Then I turn to come find you.

I walk out of the room, look left, then right, and find you standing at the back-sliding door. You are just standing there, looking out at the view. I come behind you and place a hand on the small of your back, which pulls you out of your zone.

"What are you thinking?"

"Just enjoying the view, not really thinking about anything."

"You look exhausted. You wanna lie down and take a nap for a bit?"

"I'm good. I can push through."

"You don't have to. It is only three. We have a couple of hours before we have to start thinking of what we want to do for dinner. Go take a nap."

"Are you sure? You want to join me?"

"I think I could do that," I say as I take you into the master bedroom and kick off my shoes.

You follow suit and then climb on the bed slowly until you find the center of the bed and fall over. I just watch you and smile. Then I come join you on the left side. I lie on my right side, and you turn on your side to face me. Inches from your lips, I can't help myself anymore. I slowly lean in, looking from your lips to your eyes. You just watch me.

I take my lips ever so slowly to your lips, then I pull back to look at you. I stop just shy of a couple of inches away from you, wondering if you are really that tired or if I might be able to get you energized. You take a hand to the back of my head, and I know my answer.

You pull me into you, and as our lips collide, they part ever so slightly, allowing our tongues to tease each other. The second my tongue touches yours, my heart stops beating. I move my arm from under my head to under yours and let my hand fall to your back. I take my other hand and place it on your hip, pulling you into me.

The way you are moving, I don't think you are so tired anymore. Our legs intertwine and rock back and forth with the movements of our tongue. Because I know this position isn't comfortable for long, I take advantage of the momentum our legs are creating and roll on top of you. I pull away from you, breaking our kiss once more just to look at you. I want to see what thoughts are hiding behind your eyes.

Now that both of your hands are free to move around, you curl both your arms around my back and breathlessly say, "Why did you stop?"

"I just wanted to look at you." I say as I lean back to kiss you voraciously. You take it and pull me hard against you. My hand behind your head pulls to the left and get tangled in your long hair. I drag my lips from yours to your neck and ear. As I near your ear, I let out the low moan that has been building in me since the moment our lips met. The vibration and heat of it instantly sends a chill down your body.

"I just want to kiss you for hours."

"Yes, please! What took you so long in the first place?"

"I just didn't want to rush it."

"So then, nap time was the perfect time?"

"You aren't as intimidating when your guard is down."

You just laugh in my ear, which goes right to my soul. To stop my brain from thinking, I kiss your neck and sink my teeth into the crook of your neck. Your laugh quickly turns into a pained moan. Your nails turn on me, and I know I have hit the right button. Once the pain of your nails lessens in my back, I start to release my teeth and kiss your exposed skin and move my way back up to your neck where I have moved my hand.

I slightly tilt your head, exposing the front of your neck to me. I take my tongue, and starting from the base of your neck, I lick you slowly and methodically. When I come up to your chin, I open my eyes to see you watching me. I want to know what you are thinking, but I don't want to talk anymore. So I just release your chin and kiss you once more.

We tangle ourselves up like that for the next minute or so, and then you decide it is your turn to be in control. You take your hips and throw me off balance and straddle me. You toss your hair to the side and lower yourself onto me. You slightly twist your leg to a position you know will rub against me, then you kiss me hungrily. You work your hips into mine as you continuously take my breath away.

I move my hand over your hip to your ass where I grab you tight and press you against me. You conveniently pin my other hand above my head and take your other one along my jawline to just behind my ear. Then you nibble at my lower lip and tease me with your tongue. (I could kiss you all night!)

You grab my lower lip with your teeth then gently pull away from me, allowing it to fall from your grasp as you move. You just stop inches away and look at me, like I do to you. "Why did you stop?"

"I just wanted to see what you were thinking."

"I'm thinking I don't want to stop. I am thoroughly enjoying the way you feel tangled with me. I'm also thinking if you can take my breath away with your tongue like that, what else can you do?"

With that answer, you seem satisfied because you lean in and kiss me down my neck to my collarbone, then you trace it up to my shoulder. I fully expect payback for the bite I gave you, but you don't bite me; you just nibble and kiss me. I don't know if it is the anticipation of what you can do to me or if it is what you are already doing to me that is making my breathing deepen. Whichever it is, I don't want the feeling to stop.

Then out of nowhere, you change it up and turn my head in your direction. You kiss me, and I'm helpless. My hips start moving under your weight. I free my other hand from yours and trace the lines of your back. First, down towards your ass, then back up more firmly until I reach the back of your neck. I spread my fingers and let them curl in your hair.

I hungrily kiss you until I can't take it anymore. Then I roll us again to straddle you. I pin both your hands above your head and rise up on you. Your chest is heaving with ragged inconsistency. I just look at you and smile wryly. "What?" you ask.

"Are you hungry? I'm hungry. Where are we gonna go eat?"

"What? Seriously?"

"Yeah. I've worked up an appetite." I say as I climb off the bed from between your legs. I look back at you as I walk out of the room with a wink.

"Hold up. That is it? You're hungry?"

"Yeah. We should eat something before we spend all night in bed." I say as I walk back to the bed, grab you around your hips, pull you to me and kiss you. "Don't be upset. I just wanna enjoy a little of the area before I lose myself in you. Fair warning, I'm insatiable once you get me started."

"I'm not upset. Okay, not that upset. I am just not used to people stopping. It threw me off, is all."

"Good, because I absolutely promise I will make it up to you before the end of the night."

"I am gonna hold you to that! Now, what are you hungry for?"

****

After a nice evening out where you showed me around downtown and took me to a cool place to eat, we make our way back to the condo. I haven't touched you since I pulled you off the bed. I'm waiting for you to show me what you want. Of course, that doesn't stop me from flirting all night.

When we pull into the condo's parking spot, you just shoot me a look of questioning. I just smile and get out of the car. You walk a step behind me hesitantly. I reach for the door, open it, and let you in first. You don't see the looks I give your body as you walk past me. Then I pull the door closed behind me.

When I look up from closing the door, you are standing there and watching me. "Hi," I say with a smile.

"Hi," you say with a devious smile as I walk past you into the kitchen. I resist the urge to reach out my hand to touch you as I pass by. You turn on your heels and follow me like I did something wrong. I can feel it in the way I feel your eyes on me. I don't turn around. I just get into the cabinet and pull out a glass then turn on the faucet to fill it.

When I turn the faucet off and I turn around, I find you leaning up against the opposite countertop just watching me. So I take a drink of my water and wait for you to say something or do something. I set the cup down on the counter behind me and cock my head to the right and just look at you from the floor up. You still say nothing, but by the time I look into your eyes, I see a fire burning in them.

Without saying a word, you push off hard from the counter, taking a long step towards me, which places you inches from my lips. I just smile knowingly. "What are you smiling about?"

"Just waiting to see how long it will take you to take what you want."

You don't respond, but I can see the light in your eyes change, and I know I am in for it now. You strategically place your hands on the countertop on either side of my waist and move so close that I can feel your breath on my neck along with the heat that is radiating from the rest of your body.

You take your time teasing me with your closeness. I don't move or say anything. I just wait for you. I embrace every shiver you send through me. For a moment, I can feel the soft skin of your lips graze my ear, then you move down to my exposed neckline and over to my shoulder. You quickly sink your teeth in deep and aggressively. (I should have expected that.)

My knees immediately feel weak, but the adrenaline stiffens them before they buckle. I let out a moan that I have been trying to contain. I can't control myself anymore. I have to touch you!

I take my hands off the countertop and place them firmly on your hips, then to the backside of your jeans over your ass. I pull you tight against me and bend my head into the crook of your neck. I nip at your skin, then kiss you behind your ear. You release your bite and seem to lose yourself in what my lips are doing. I stop and pull back to the front of your ear. "Took you long enough."

You pull back from me and just look at me with wild flames in your eyes. I take a hand off your ass and place it firmly in your hair. Gripping you hard, I claim your lips with mine. I aggressively kiss you until our bodies have heated up to the point where we are so damn hot that I have to take your clothes off.

You have resisted the urge to touch me until then, digging your nails into the countertop. Now you take your hands straight to my waistband and unbutton my shorts, dropping them to the floor, and then you place your hands firmly on my stomach and slide them up my shirt to my breasts. You firmly grip them and massage them while I work your jeans off and begin dragging your shirt up from the back. I force you to stop so I can remove it.

That doesn't stop you for long though. Once your hands are free from your shirt, you quickly move to remove mine. Except you don't take mine all the way off. You tie up my hands behind me with it and pull me away from the counter and out of my shorts that are at my feet. With my hands behind my back, you are in complete control of me. (Holy shit, what a turn on!)

You force me to stand in between the counters to the center of the kitchen. You size me up slowly from head to toe. (Luckily, I am in my flip flops because I would have felt very awkward if I am in nothing but my underwear and shoes.) You give me a sly smile as you step to me with your hands perched precariously at my chest. Then you methodically place your hands just below my bra and glide them under it. Your fingers circle my breast until your index fingers and thumbs pinch my nipples. As I start to moan, you kiss me, stealing my breath and stopping my heart.

I feel all the blood in my body rush to between my thighs. The heat of our bodies is causing me to fight my instincts of freeing myself and taking you. You tease me with your hands, then push your hands up to either side of my neck, dragging my bra with them. For a moment, my bra stops me from breathing because of the slight pressure. Then you lift it over my head and down over my shoulders to join my shirt at my hands. You kiss me down my throat to my right nipple where you tease me with your tongue. You circle around it, then eclipse it with your mouth, sucking and biting it.

"Ah god, the things you make me feel with that mouth of yours!"

You don't stop, but I feel you smile against me. I squirm under your touch. I don't know how much more I can take. Then you turn your attention to the waistband of my underwear. While your mouth is busy, your hands glide over my hip bones, pushing my underwear down over my ass and exposing my tattoos. You catch a glimpse of them and stop teasing my nipple. You kiss your way down my navel to my tattoos, where you allow your fingers to trace over one and take your tongue over the other. (Oh fuck, I'm gonna lose it!)

You moan against my navel then kiss me. You readjust yourself to a kneeling position in front of me and look up at me. I can't bring myself to do anything except watch you. Without taking your eyes off me, you hook your fingers in my waistband and pull my underwear down slowly to the floor. You lean to the right and begin kissing my hip bone, then you follow its line downwards. I'm pretty sure I stopped breathing again.

Then out of nowhere, you take your tongue and drag it up my navel, past my breasts, and up the side of my neck as you stand up before me. "Why did you stop?" I said, finally being able to breathe again.

"'Cause I'm not done punishing you for earlier."

I just smiled, knowing I so deserve this. "Now stay there."

"Yes, ma'am."

You take a couple of steps away from me, then you stop. You smile, then you reach up and begin removing your bra, followed with your underwear, allowing them to fall to the floor at your feet. I just bite my lower lip thinking of all the things I want to do to you and of all the places I want to kiss and touch. But I don't move. I wait to see where you are taking this. You watch me as I take in the sight of you.

I don't realize it until you walk up to me and take your thumb over my lower lip that I have been biting it the whole time. Then you kiss me impatiently, pressing your naked body against mine. (I can't help myself; I may not be able to use my hand, but—help me GOD—I am gonna use my lips and tongue!)

I break our kiss and start kissing your collarbone, then I make my way down your chest. I have no control over you, so it is at your pleasure and leisure of what I am able to do to you. You don't move, though, so I move over your left breast and kiss your nipple softly, then I swirl my tongue around it and nip at it until I steady myself enough that I can wrap my mouth around it without falling into you. You feel my hesitation, so you move closer to me.

With pleasure, I moan into you as the feel of your nipple harden for me between my lips, releasing the intensity that has been building in my chest. I need more, though, so I release you and make my way down your navel. You place a hand on the top of my head and grip a chunk of hair, pulling my head back, forcing me to look up at you. I just give you a hungry look and pull my head closer to your navel. You keep the pressure on my head trying to fight me. I just reach out my tongue and lick you near your mound.

You lighten up the pressure and allow me to kiss you. Then you take a step to your left and pull me into you. I don't miss a beat; I react to you like a thirsty man in a desert that just found an inch of water. I savor your taste; the salt warms my blood. I want to touch you with my hand, but I resist. I allow my tongue to dance around your throbbing clit.

Every once in a while, I wrap my lips around it and suckle you until you moan. Then I release you and flatten my tongue over you. You know exactly what I am trying to do, so you help me by pulling me harder into you. You grind your hips into me. (That's it, I can't take it anymore!)

In a single swift movement, I release my hands and throw them between your legs to your firm ass, forcing you to widen your stance. I reposition myself and grip your ass hard. Pulling you into me with such ferocity that you almost lose your balance. I make you widen your stance further by using my elbows between your thighs. I lighten the pressure over your clit to tease your hole with my tongue. I need to taste more of you.

Without warning I take a hand from your ass and slide a couple of fingers inside of you. You gasp and moan as my fingers begin thrusting in and out of you. Now, you have placed both your hands on my head, begging me for more. I can feel you about to cum. I know you need the release. Your body tenses at the pressure change of my tongue. When I feel you can't take anymore, I take my fingers to the backside of your clit and send you over the top.

"YES, yes, don't stop! PLEASE DON'T . . . STOP!"

On that note, I turn my nails into your ass and drag them down the backside of your leg. Simultaneously, I pull my fingers from inside of you to my lips still covering your clit. (This is gonna be a fantastic night!)

As I taste you on my fingers, I moan and stand up in front of you, allowing my other hand to drag up your inner thigh, around your hip, and to the small of your back. I slowly pull my fingers from between my curling lips. You look at me with heavy lids as your hands release my hair and fall to my shoulders. I quickly wrap my hand around the back of your neck and pull you into me, kissing you seductively. Your hands snake their way around my body to my back.

I move you over to the counter and press your back up against it. Then I quickly drop both my hands to your ass and lift you on top of it, breaking our kiss. You look at me with wander. I just smile and whisper against your lips, "I told you I am insatiable once you get me started."

And with that said, I take the palm of my right hand and place it in the middle of your chest, pressing it backwards until you are forced to throw your hands behind you to catch yourself from falling. My hand firmly rise up to your neck, just under your chin. I slightly turn your head to the left and lean into you, pressing myself into your wetness.

I slowly move my hips between your legs, grinding my mound into yours while I take my time tracing your neckline with my tongue and lips. "Oh god, that feels so good. Don't stop," you say breathlessly. I take my hand, grip your hair tight, and pull your head back as I thrust hard into you. You let out a moan in my ear, breaking my concentration.

I slowly take my tongue up your neck and off your chin to watch you. I use my other hand to hold you on the edge of the countertop. Your eyes look heavy, and your body is moving like it is ready for something a little more intense, so I move my hand around your hip until it sits firmly between our wet pussies. I turn my palm inward and allow a couple of fingers to penetrate you. I keep grinding into you harder and harder as my fingers vibrate inside of you.

You snap your head up to mine and kiss me with so much hunger that I can't deny your tongue. I welcome its coolness. Your breath catches when I lean into you. Our tongues dance around each other teasingly. I hold you against me when I feel your body tense beneath my arms. (Oh no, you don't!) I quickly stop moving every part of my body except my tongue. You moan into my mouth, begging for me to resume pleasuring you, but I resist until I feel your desperation.

Pulling away from your lips, I softly nip at your lower lip. Then I work my way down your tight body until your navel with my lips. I stop and look up at you. Your eyes are begging me to finish you off. I look from your eyes to your lips. They are a little puffy from our kiss and are slightly parted. Then I drop my gaze to your chest, heaving with every deep breath you try to catch.

I take a hand under a leg and lift it to rest on my shoulder. Then I take the other one and do the same, allowing the weight of your legs to push me to my knees. I kiss your inner thigh with a deliberately slow tenderness to tease you. Moving methodically, I turn my head so close to your hardened clit to allow the heat of my breath to warm you, then I look the other direction into your other thigh and kiss it until I hear you almost whimper.

I smile at you taking the hint, and I resume my position over your clit. I look up at you and see you watching my movements with extreme intensity. I slightly part my lips and press my tongue forward and down the front of your clit until you feel the full pressure of it. You close your eyes and throw your head back as the pleasure of my tongue shoots through your body.

I close my eyes and take your scent in, wrapping my lips around your hardness. My tongue begins to circle and flick around you in a dance with an intensifying pressure and purpose. (Now, I need to make you cum for me.)

I feel you press your hips into me, begging for more. More pressure, more intensity. I eagerly rise to meet your body's demands. To send you over the top, I begin sucking you into my mouth. That does it, and your body goes ridged in front of me. I continue sucking until your orgasm takes over your body. Then I lighten the intensity and dance lightly around your clit while welcoming the taste of your pleasure.

I hold you tight until I feel you can't take it anymore, then I pull back, allowing your clit to slip from my mouth. With both of my arms wrapped around your legs, I look up at you and smile. You slide your hips back so you are firmly sitting on the countertop, then you take both your hand to the sides of my face and pull me up towards you, letting your legs fall to my sides.

You pull me into a kiss. At first, our lips caress softly, then something clicks in you, and your hunger is back. You take a hand to the back of my head, pulling me hard against you. I, of course, welcome your passion and meet it as my breathing deepens and my heart begins to race. I don't know what you have planned or what clicked in you, but I'm very excited to find out.

You move both your hands to my chest and slowly move them over my breasts until you pause just above my nipples. Then unexpectedly, you shove me away from you. I stumble back to the counter behind me and brace myself in shock. You hop off the counter and look me up and down, then you pause on my hips. When you make whatever decision you are contemplating, you look up at me and stride over to me.

You firmly take both your hands to my hips and kiss me hard, then in one swift motion, you spin me around, so I am facing the window looking out over the ocean. I feel your hands tracing the curves of my body, then one moves to my hip bone and the other seems to move with your body as you take a step between my legs.

I turn to look at you, but you quickly move your hand to the back of my head and force me to look away. Then I feel you press your wet body against mine. First, I feel your mound press hard against my ass, then your midsection and breasts as they press against my shoulders. Then I feel you stop with your lips so close to the back of my neck that I can feel your hot breath teasing me.

I relax under your pressure until I feel your hand leave my hip and work its way forward over my navel, then down between the counter and my wet pussy. I feel all the blood in my body chase after your hand. Just as your fingertips curl over my throbbing clit, you kiss the back of my neck. I instantly stop breathing.

You take the hand at the back of my neck and move my head to the side and kiss me under my ear, sending chills throughout my body. Then you dip your fingers deep inside me, causing me to resume breathing. (God, you feel so good inside me!)

You notice the change in my body and stop kissing me for a moment, if for nothing else but to tease me more. "You don't get to have all the fun tonight," you say in a breathy whisper.

"Ah gods, you are gonna torture me all night, aren't you?"

"Maybe. Depends on how well you cum for me."

I can't speak—all that comes out from me is a moan. You curl your fingers deep and use the palm of your hand to apply pressure to my already hardened clit. I can feel your fingers thrumming inside of me. I can't help it; I move my hips into you, pressing my ass against your already wet pussy. You moan into my ear then turn my head to reach my lips. I use the leverage I have against the countertop to keep the pressure against you. You curl your fingers in my hair in approval.

You quicken your palm movements to spur on my orgasm. It really isn't gonna take much. Touching you and pleasing you has me so freaking excited that I'm surprised I haven't cum for you yet. And just like that, the moment the thought hits me, you bite my lip and break out a kiss. You press hard into me from the front and the back, then you find the sweet spot on the back of my neck and massage it with your tongue and lips. (OH GOD, I am so gonna cum!)

Within moments, I feel the shock wave shoot through my body to my pleading wetness. As I begin to spasm, I feel your body tense behind me. "Fuck, YES, don't stop!"

You stop kissing me, then say, "Oh GOD, I couldn't if I wanted to. YES, yes, I'm coming, I'm coming!" which makes me want to intensify my movement against you even more. You pull me against you while I grind, taking us both over the edge for as long as we can last. "Oh god, I can't, honey. We have to stop. Please, I can't take it anymore."

And with my pleading, you slow your movements with mine and gently withdraw your fingers from inside me. You kiss me against the back of my neck, making me shiver once more, then you spin me and kiss me. "Now, this is a vacation I could get used to!"

THUNDERSTORM

We're sitting on the porch at sunset, watching the lightning and listening to the thunder roll. We cuddle on a blanket at the top of the stairs. (You feel so good in my arms that I need to kiss you.) I roll my body towards you, placing your head on the bend in my arm and kiss you. You meet my lips with yours softly. The passion builds between us as our tongues dance around us.

(My turn!) You drag your hand up my arm to my shoulder, where I expect you to pull me harder into you, and you shove me hard onto my back, pinning me to the floor. You look at me with a hunger I've never seen before. I try to rise up to kiss you, but you just press me harder into the boards. I look up at you questioningly, and as if you read my thoughts, you smirk and lean down into my neck and begin teasing me with your bites.

Your teeth send powerful shivers and heat waves throughout my body. I give in to you, enjoying your breath, your tongue, and your teeth as they stimulate all of my senses. You make your way up the side of my neck, behind my ear, and back down my neck to my shoulder. You lovingly linger over my shoulder, enjoying every inch of it.

(I can't take this anymore—I need to touch you. I need to feel your heart race under my kiss.) I struggle under you for a moment till you give me that little opening, and I wrestle you to your back. I pin you down and kiss you so hard you can feel my desire.

I take my right hand from your wrist down to your thigh and slide my hand over it and up your side till I reach your breast. I move my lips and make my way to your neck. I kiss you behind your ear and down to your shoulder.

I grind my hips into you teasingly. (Oh my god, I love the way your hips feel when they move over me! I know I can't take much more of this. I'm going to cum all over your fingers the minute you slide them into me!) Your arms wrap around my chest and pull me down tight against you. I bite your neck, and you dig your nails into my back in response to the intensity of my teeth. (Fuck me! You know just where to touch me to make me go crazy! I don't know how much more I can take!)

I release my bite and arch my back. I thrust my hips hard into you. You kiss, then bite my neck, demonstrating to me how much I have gotten to you. You roll me over and pin me down once again. You taunt me with your lips, lightly tracing them over mine and down the front of my neck. I struggle and thrust my hips upwards, trying to create a little room for me to maneuver so I can take control again.

You lose your balance and I overcome you. (Ha-ha, it worked.) The lightning strikes behind me, lighting up the sky. I pause for a moment, and then I stand up and offer my hand to you. You take it and stand up. I wrap my arms around you. In a tight embrace, we kiss as the thunder begins to roll over the sky above, sending pounding vibrations through us. You lead me inside, grabbing a blanket. We go to the fireplace, where you lay the blanket down.

I come from behind you, gliding my hand firmly under your shirt, and around the front of your pants. I press my pelvis into your ass as my other hand wraps around your hips and press your body upright. I undo your belt and pants with a quickness and need.

Once I have your pants open to me, I take my left hand up under your shirt to your breast. I massage your breast over your bra and slide my other hand between your underwear and your soft skin. My hand moves towards the heat of your pussy and settles over your clit.

My lips drag against the back of your neck to your shoulder. The heat of my breath lingers over your skin where my lips pass. I flick my tongue out at your skin and sink my teeth deep into your shoulder. Your breathing quickens, and your hips begin rotating with hunger. (Fuck, YES! God, I hope you press your fingers inside me soon. I need to cum. I want to cum all over your fingers.) You arch your back and press your ass hard against me. The pressure of my hand intensifies on your clit.

(God, I'm so torn. I want you to make me cum. I also want to taste you and see how wet you've become!)

Then out of nowhere, you turn to face me. You rip my shirt and bra off in one aggressive motion. You begin kissing me and biting my lower lip. Your hands don't go to my back this time; this time, they slide down my chest; nails dragging down my skin to my navel. Then your hands relax enough to undo my pants and tear them down my legs. You drop to your knees to kneel in front of me.

(Oh my god, YES! This is so fucking hot. You are so gorgeous on your knees.) The light from the fire makes your skin glow with such a softness.

You lean into my naked body and kiss my inner thigh. Your hands glide up the back of my legs to my ass. You pull me close and tight as you tease me with your kisses. "God, you are so beautiful, baby! I love you and your lips!" Then you pull me to the floor and climb on top of me.

"I love you too, babe!" you say as you straddle me and begin grinding your hips. I reach up and pull your shirt off while pulling you to me. I unlatch your bra and slide my hands down your back as you throw your bra to the floor.

My hands slide under the backside of your pants, and I grab your ass as you continue to grind into me. Your naked boobs press against mine as you lean in and kiss me. (I love the feel of your skin touching mine!) Breaking our kiss, you start licking and kissing your way down my body.

You pause at my boobs and begin sucking and nibbling my nipples. "Uuuuuhhhh . . . mmmmm," is all I can manage to get out as the pleasure began to overwhelm me. I lick my lips just thinking about what is going to happen in the next few minutes.

You take your hand down my side and over my hip. You push your way between our two bodies, cup your hand, and press your fingers on my clit.

Your fingers begin to flick around my clit. Your pelvis applies pressure to your hand while my breathing becomes heavy and I start moaning. Your lips release my nipple, and your tongue slides down my body. You make your way down my legs as I spread them, welcoming you.

You bite my inner thigh when you reach my pussy. You take your fingers down between my engorged lips and into my wetness. You begin moving inside me as your tongue finds my clit. (God, yes, right there. Don't move, right there . . . that feels so good!)

"God, that feels so good. Don't stop!"

You moan over my clit in response to my breathless words.

Pressing your tongue down flat and hard on my clit, you pulse it. Your fingers press under my clit, flicking your fingers with intensity and need. You lighten the pressure of your tongue and begin to flick and circle around my clit.

You speed up and intensify your tongue and fingers once more, confusing my body, making my heart pound with intensity and greed. My body begins to tense, and my back starts to arch. You slide your other hand up my stomach, pause for a moment, then you drag your nails downward as I begin coming.

"Yes, FUCK, YES! I'm coming. Don't stop, baby!" I say as I reach for you. Every muscle in my body tenses from the intensity of my orgasm. You begin lightening the pressure of your tongue until I relax beneath you. Then you slide up, over the top of me, until you reach my lips. My body spasms with aftershocks until the full weight of your body presses down on me. You kiss me softly. I smile, then I wrap my arms around you, and roll you onto your back.

I slide my naked body over the top of yours and kiss your neck. Your hands grip my shoulders and hold me tight to your body. I sink my teeth into your neck. Your nails start to dig, enjoying the pain my teeth are shooting through you.

A moment later, I relinquish my teeth's grip and slide my tongue down your chest to one of your nipples. I wrap my lips around your nipple and suck and tease you with my tongue until you begin moaning.

I release your nipple when I feel your breathing become labored and continue my way down your body, kissing and licking you all over. My hands find their way down to your legs. One wraps around your thigh and the other slides between your wet lips.

(God, you are so hard! This won't take too long if I do it right. Nah, I wanna play a little!)

My fingers torment your clit as I tease you with my tongue. You ask me, "Please!" I like how you said the word "please." I press my fingers inside your wet, writhing pussy. I push deep inside of you till I cannot press any further.

You start to scream with pleasure. My tongue guides my way to your throbbing clit. My lips wrap around it and my tongue flicks. You try not to dig your nails into my arm wrapped around your leg.

The pressure from within deepens with every stroke of my fingers. My tongue intensifies and then lightens as your hips grind below me. I thrust harder and harder. Your screams begin to choke off to a silence.

I lighten the pressure and quicken my movements. You find your voice and begin to cum while I lightly circle your clit.

(Fuck the teasing—I NEED to make you cum!) Instead of releasing my grip on you, I strengthen it. I continue licking and sucking your clit and withdraw my fingers so I can use both my arms to pull you into me. You grip my hair, pulling me towards you, increasing my pressure on your clit. My tongue slides up and down between your lips. I circle your hole and tease it. You scream out, "Fuck me!" and that is all I needed to hear.

I take my hand back around your leg and slide my fingers hard inside of you. I take my tongue off your clit and drag it up to your navel. I raise my head and look at you, and I smirk. I brace myself above you and allow my pelvis to assist the motions of my fingers inside of you. The palm of my hand presses against your clit. I thrust in and out of your hot, wet pussy, begging your body to cum all over my hand.

Your hips fall into rhythm with mine. I rotate my hips as you thrust. Your breathing deepens and becomes raspy as I lean down to kiss you. You tuck your head between my neck and my shoulder out of fear that I will totally take your breath away, so we kiss each other's necks.

As the thrusting of our hips intensifies, we both sink our teeth in. You begin coming once again, but I don't let up; instead, I fuck you harder. (I love making you cum and tasting you!) You cum all over my hand. Only when you start to collapse to the floor do I stop. I slide my fingers gently out of you. Laying you down, I lay myself on top of you and kiss you. I take a moment to take in the sight of the firelight glistening off our naked bodies.

FRUSTRATIONS RELEASED

After a long week all I want is a nice, relaxing bath and some sort of release. The drive home seems to be taking forever! Finally, I arrive home. I fumble for my keys and open the door to an empty, quiet house.

I walk through the kitchen and down the dark hall to the bathroom. I begin running the hot water. Once the water gets to the perfect temperature, I return to the kitchen to find a bottle of wine. I grab a goblet and pour myself a nice full glass. Taking a relaxing sip, I turn and walk back to the bathroom.

Setting the glass on the corner of the tub, I begin to undress while the tub finishes filling, leaving my clothes in a pile where they fall off my body. I light some candles and place them around the tub. Before climbing into the tub, I walk back to the door and turn off the light. I return to the tub, turn off the water, and gently step in. I sink into the hot water, as my thoughts wash away.

I finish off the glass of wine, close my eyes, and wish the steam to wash my frustrations away. My hands drift down my body. I mindlessly begin touching myself. I realize this is exactly the release I need.

A moment later, I hear you come in through the kitchen door. You come down the hall into the bathroom. Before you begin talking, you see my eyes closed and the water moving over my hand as I rub my clit.

You watch me for a moment till I begin opening my eyes. "Sorry, I didn't mean to interrupt you," you say with a smile. I look at you and smile. I remove my hand and climb out of the tub. With the water dripping from my body, I reach for my towel casually. I begin drying myself as I watch you watching me. I wrap the towel around myself and step to you. I kiss you softly at first. My hands wrap around you and down your back.

With your embrace, my towel falls to the floor. My heart begins to race. I reach down, over your ass to the top of your thighs. I lift you and you wrap your legs around my naked body. You smile.

I turn your back to the wall thinking of letting out my frustrations on you. Kissing you hard, I take a hand and slide it down the back of your shorts. I grab your ass forcefully, breaking our kiss. I trail my tongue down your throat. I kiss your collarbone softly.

I breathe heavily on your neck as my tongue sends shivers down your back. You tilt your head back, welcoming my touch. I sink my teeth deep into your skin as your nails dig through the skin on my back.

I thrust my pelvis into yours. You moan loudly into my ear. I release my bite as your head tilts towards mine. We kiss. I reach my hand down to undo your shorts.

Your nails lighten on my skin. While I undo your pants, you caress my back and the back of my head. Our kiss deepens. I slide my hand between our pelvises and touch your clit. I feel your pulse throb beneath my fingers. You break our kiss and whisper, "Yes!"

I kiss you harder. Our tongues dance like we can't get enough of each other. My fingers rotate around your clit as my pelvis thrusts and grinds into you.

I break our kiss and look into your eyes as my fingers lighten and slide between your wet lips. They glide with ease inside of you. With a deep breath, I hear you say "Yes" again, but this time it sounds more wanting.

My fingers penetrate deeper into you. The palm of my hand smacks into you with every thrust of my hips. I lean into you, kissing your neck as you kiss mine.

I move faster inside of you, yearning for your screams. Soon enough, you pierce my ears with your loud, tantalizing screams of elation and rapture.

I thrust harder till you can't take it anymore. Your breathing slows as your body goes limp in my arms. You quiver against the wall. I withdraw my fingers slowly from deep inside of you. I wrap my arms around you, kissing your neck tenderly. I glide you down the wall to the floor.

Your legs are still wrapped around my waist. I sit on the floor under you. I hold you tight as your body's shivers dissipate.

You kiss my neck softly. My hands delicately caress your back. They trail down to your ass, where I grip both cheeks firmly and kiss you with renewed intensity.

(I don't feel satisfied yet.)

I feel your pussy pulsating and dripping against mine. I begin to lift you into a standing position above me. As your body lifts off me, I kiss you down to your navel.

I drop my hands from your ass and slide myself to the other side of the doorway. I reach for you and entice you to come to me. You move within inches away from my face.

My hands wrap their way around your thighs. I stare hungrily at your wet, glistening pussy. I pull you onto my face. I kiss your engorged lips. My tongue slides between them, finding your pulsating clit.

You drop a hand down to the back of my head in approval. Gripping my hair, you force me deeper into you. Your other hand is against the door frame, bracing your body.

"Don't stop!" is all I heard.

I intensify my purpose-driven tongue. My hands rise to grip your ass once again. I pull you over my face. Your breathing deepens, and your moans increase in intensity and frequency.

You tell me, "FUCK ME!" So I take a hand from your ass, dragging it teasingly down the back of your quivering thigh and up the inside of it. I pause just shy of your pussy, making you beg for it.

After a moment, I finally give in. I turn my hand towards the ceiling, and cupping a hand under my chin, I lightly slip two fingers between your throbbing lips. They easily penetrate into your wetness.

I thrust hard and deep inside of you. Your moans turn into screams. Your fingers twist in my hair, pulling harder. (God, I can't get enough!)

My fingers stroke and flick inside your tightening pussy, as my tongue lightens and begins to circle your clit. You begin yelling, "Yes! Right there! Don't stop!"

I continue my movements but increase my speed. You go silent, your breathing pauses, and your hand presses hard at the back of my head. I feel your pussy tightens around my fingers.

I suckle your clit as my tongue strokes the softness around your engorged clit. Just as your body begins to tremble, I fuck you harder.

"Oh yes! Fuck, yes! Don't stop! Fuck me, don't STOP!" you scream in ecstasy.

I persist. You become breathless. You take your hand from the back of my head to my forehead. Feeling the pressure of your hand, I release my lip's embrace.

(I want more!)

My fingers glide from inside you. I wrap my arms around your waist. I look up and kiss your navel. Then I turn my head, leaning it against your body, and enjoy the momentary embrace.

Your heartbeat is racing, and your breathing calms. You gently caress my head, letting your nails lightly graze my skin.

Once your pulse slows, you step back and extend your hand. I take it and stand up. You lead me from the bathroom down the hallway, towards the bedroom.

I'm still feeling like my release is incomplete.

I still crave more of you. I release your hand and step behind you. Desiring to touch your soft skin, I grab your waist, stopping you mid-stride. I pull you back to me.

I turn you to face the wall. My one hand slides down your hip bone and around to your lower back. I glide it up your spine, intensifying the pressure as my hand reaches the back of your head. I force you to bend into the wall.

Your hands reach out to either side of you to brace yourself. I hear you catch your breath. My other hand reaches in between your legs. My palm presses firmly against your lips.

You turn to one side to watch me. Lightening the pressure on your upper back, I trace the lines of your back, admiring the beauty of you. The sweat makes your skin glisten in the light of the candles still flickering around the bathtub.

You take a hand and place it over mine, between your legs. You move my hand back and forth over your pussy. I feel your pulse quicken under the weight of our hands.

You press harder over my middle and index fingers, forcing them to penetrate you. I slowly push deeper into you. With immense pressure, I tantalize your clit with my palm.

I bring my other hand under your arm to your breast. I grasp it aggressively as you moan loudly. I massage it and tease your nipple with my fingers, pinching and twisting them.

I slide my fingers in and out of your pussy methodically, lightly. You grow desperate and impatient. You urgently whisper, "Please." I know just what you want.

I take my hand from your breast, lightly dragging it to your back and up to your neck. I take a step closer to you and press my pussy against your ass.

In one aggressive, fluent movement, my hand wraps around your neck, under your chin, forcing your head to tilt back. My hips slams into your ass, forcing my fingers deep and hard inside of you. Your breasts press firmly against the cold wall, hardening your nipples.

I fuck you hard enough that your screams of complete rapture are barely a hoarse whisper. My pussy repeatedly slams into you with every movement of my hips.

(Yes, this is what I need!)

The speed of my hips quickens. My pussy throbs, my pulse races, and my breathing deepens. You grow silent, your breathing is deep, and your sounds are forced. I lightly tighten my grip as my fingers intensify their movements inside of you.

You begin to shiver as my knees grow weak. We both cum until our bodies can't take it anymore. I release my grip on your neck, placing my hand against the wall for balance. I withdraw my hand from between your legs gently.

I wrap my arms around your waist and kiss the back of your neck, sending shivers down your back. I collapse into you as we both catch our breath.

With a strong exhale, I feel my frustrations get released. We fall to the floor in an embrace and fall asleep where we lay.

MOVIE NIGHT

You come over to watch a movie while my roommate is out of town. I have you pick a movie while I watch you from the couch. You are wearing a thin, almost see-through, black shirt, with a black and red checkered skirt. (You're so hot right now!)

I lie with my back to the arm of the couch, facing the TV. You put the movie on and join me. I spread my legs, welcoming you to cuddle with me. You lie firmly between my legs, with your head just above my breasts. I wrap my arms around you, pulling you close. You lightly lay a hand on my arm, appreciating my touch.

About halfway through the movie, you get up and go to the bathroom. I wait a moment before getting up. (I can't stand this anymore!) I meet you outside my bedroom door. I slide one hand around your hips and the other up the back of your neck. I wrap my fingers in your hair and back your body to the wall, kissing you passionately.

You wrap your arms around my body and pull me tightly against you. I lose my breath as your kiss catches me off guard. My hand glides under your shirt and along your back. I feel your body quiver under my soft touch. You take one hand down to the doorknob. You slowly turn the knob, like you are having a difficulty in kissing me and opening the door at the same time. Finally, the door unlatches and swings open.

I take you off the wall, picking you up as we move. I throw you on the bed. You let out a teasing moan. I climb on top of you, wanting to really take control. You tear my shirt off me like it is on fire. I grab the bottom of your shirt and pull it over your head with just as much enthusiasm.

I place one leg between yours, and leaning down, I press my breasts against yours. Your thin lace bra allows me to feel your nipples harden under mine. I kiss you softly as the weight of my thigh presses against your silk underwear, lightly veiling your pussy. Our kisses become deeply intense. I grind into you harder and faster. I feel my breath deepen, and my pulse race with pure adrenaline in anticipation of what is to come. You grip the back of my shoulders with both hands.

I can feel each of your fingers pushing into my skin. I begin teasing you with my lips, and I let them lightly touch yours. My tongue slides between your lips, grazing over your tongue and out again. I bite your lower lip playfully. You moan in a way that lets me know that you like what I'm doing to you.

My teeth lighten enough to allow your lip to slip from my mouth. I kiss you fully, then I drag my tongue over your chin and down the front of your neck to kiss your collarbone.

As I guide my lips and my tongue up the side of your neck, your nails begin digging into my back. You let a moan out as goose bumps start rising up all over your body. I react to you by sinking my teeth into your neck, just below your ear. Your moans deepen, and your nails dig in deeper as you drag them down my back.

I release my bite and raise my head, feeling a mixture of both pleasure and pain. I look into your eyes for a second, trying to read you. You look at me with a hunger I have never seen before. I lean down to kiss you. Your nails withdraw from my back as your arms softly embrace me. You roll me to my back and mount me as if I am going to escape.

My hands slide up your back and begin undoing your bra. You place your hands on my breasts, gripping them hard. Your fingers wrap around the bottom of my bra and tear it over my head. My heart races faster with anticipation for what you'll do next; my mind whirls.

Your breasts graze my lips as you tie my wrists together with my bra. I adjust my head and take your nipple into my mouth. My teeth bite down softly as I begin sucking. You moan in my ear as you feel my teeth on your skin. My tongue traces over and around your nipple.

You sink lower into me, wanting more. One hand stays on my wrists, while the other arm wraps around my head. You moan with a heavy breath into my ear, then you bite me. I release your breast, wanting so much to feel your tongue against mine. You slid your naked breasts down over mine.

You glide one hand down my arm and over my chest, tracing the curves of my body. Your other hand grabs and lightly pulls my hair, tilting my head back and making my back arch slightly. Your tongue glides down my neck and over my breast bone. You grip my breast as your mouth falls over my nipple.

You inhale deeply as you suck my nipple into your mouth. Your tongue flicks my nipple. You take your hand from my breast and over my navel. I begin moaning softly. (I want to move my hands; I want to touch your soft skin.) Your hand pushes past our hips. I want to scream, "Oh YES! Please touch me!" but I don't; instead, I just wait silently for you to do what you want to me.

You press your fingers against my clit, making me moan with a hunger I never knew I possessed. My arms find their way over my head to your back. I can't restrain myself anymore. I pull you deeper into me. Your fingers twist and turn over my pussy. I grind my hips towards yours, pressing your fingers harder on me. (I want you inside of me!)

I can't take it anymore. I thrust my hips hard to one side and roll us over as one. On top of you, I pull my hands up under your back and over your head.

I manage to untie my hands by squirming them free. I pin yours to the bed above your head and kiss you hard. Taking one hand down over your breast, I leave the other hand to keep you restrained. I continue moving my hand down your body, over your navel to the top of your pants. I feel your chest rise and fall under my body with every deep breath you take. I feel your breathing coming harder as I undo the button and slowly unzip your pants.

I slide my other hand off your wrists as I pull away from your wanting lips. Crawling my way down your body, I slide between your legs and onto the floor. Bending over to you, my hands wrap around either side of your pants. I pull your pants and underwear off in one aggressive move as I stand between your legs.

I kiss my way up your now bare legs. My hands glide up the side of your thighs as I climb back on the bed. You quiver once again to the touch of my hands. The pressure of my fingers and hands intensifies as they approach your hips. One hand glides over your hip and stops at your navel. The other hand makes its way to your breast as my tongue reaches for your throbbing clit.

I feel your clit throb against the pressure of my tongue. I feel your pulse pounding under my touch with every movement I make. Your hips writhe beneath me. I wrap my lips around your clit and suck it into my mouth. I flick my tongue around it, teasing you. You begin screaming. I tease you a little, and then you beg for me to fuck you.

I release your clit and kiss my way up your body. My right hand slides between your legs. I press hard as it makes its way over your clit to your wet, wanting pussy. My fingers press inside you. I kiss you hard as my fingers penetrate you repeatedly, aggressively.

Just as I am really getting enthralled, you break away from my kiss. Your breathing becomes sporadic. You grip my back hard, digging your nails into me. I quicken the speed of my thrusts and flick my fingers into your G-spot. I feel you begin to cum before I actually hear your screams.

I press harder and deeper into you until your orgasm fades. I gently withdraw my fingers from your now cum-ridden pussy. Your body twitches below mine, so I press my body fully against yours. With a sense of pride, I smirk at you as I lean in to kiss you.

You thrust your hips up and roll me onto my back just as I can feel your hot breath on my lips. You linger over me, smirking. I can tell your mind is racing. This wipe the smirk off my face as I contemplate what is about to happen to me.

You perch yourself seductively over me. Your lips are just inches away from mine. Your breasts barely graze my nipples. I feel your pussy dripping over mine.

Slowly, you lean into me. Your lips brush over mine. I try to kiss you, but you turn your head. Your cheek lightly touches mine as you move your hips down and back. I feel your breath tickle my ear. You whisper, "Do you like the feel of my wet pussy on yours?"

I try to speak, but I can't. It feels like my heart is beating in my throat, so I just nod. (This is so fucking HOT!) You say nothing more. I can tell you are smiling. Your cheek is pressing harder against mine. I close my eyes for a second to take in the moment. I try to focus my thoughts. I try to make myself speak.

Before I can manage to do any of those things, I feel you move. Your lips press against mine; they are soft and slightly open. My lips naturally react, as does my heart rate. I try to catch my breath between kisses but can't.

For a moment, I thought the temperature of our night had softened. But just as the thought entered my head, you bite my lower lip and take my hands. You pick them up and slam them on the mattress above my head. (God, yes. Finally, a woman who can take control of me!)

Your hips pulsate on mine. Your wet clit rubs against my needing clit. My eyes open, mainly out of curiosity. Our eyes meet. I try to decipher what I see in your eyes. I can't. All I can interpret is intensity and complete rapture in whatever plans you have come up with.

I try to struggle for a minute under the weight of your hands, but you just tighten your grip and press me harder into the bed. I feel my pussy grow wetter as you rub against my clit. You kiss and nibble my neck, sending shivers down my spine.

I start moaning with pleasure. You change your hip movements from the back and forth motions to rotational grinding. You loosen your grip on my wrists and gracefully lift your torso up off mine.

Before your full weight is on my pelvis, you lean down, gently pressing your lips to mine. Your tongue slides past our lips and tangles with mine, giving me butterflies. I want more, so I throw my arms around your shoulders.

I bring my hand up to the back of your head, gently entwining my fingers in your hair. I pull you deeper into me, attempting to keep you there forever, but you sense my intentions and pull away.

You kiss your way down my body. When you reach my navel, your lips cease to touch me. I raise my head to see what you're doing. You just smile. Then you thrust the rest of your body between my legs.

You wrap your arms under my thighs and rest your hands on my pelvic bones. As you duck your head into my pussy, I drop my head back to the bed and close my eyes. I let out a pleasurable gasp as I feel your tongue press against my pulsating clit. (Fuck, yes!)

Your tongue circulates and flicks at my clit. Occasionally, I feel your tongue slide between my lips and rim my hole, teasing me. I feel myself wanting more, so I tell you to put your fingers inside of me. (I need to feel you inside of me.)

You drag a hand over my hip and under my thigh. I feel your fingers easily glide between my lips as your mouth continues teasing my clit.

Your fingers thrust hard into my eager pussy. I let out a loud moan as I feel you completely inside of me, finding my sweet spot.

I feel my deep breaths becoming erratic and the blood draining from my limbs to gather in my pussy. I know any minute I could cum. I feel your tongue flick just the right spot on my clit. I scream out, "Yes, right there! Oh yes! Don't stop!"

You listen to my words and hear the urgency in my tone. You know I'm close, so you continue your tongue movements and intensify your finger penetration.

I feel a wash come over me as I begin coming on your fingers. My legs tighten around your head. My pelvis convulses under your mouth. I grip the sheets on either side of me, tearing at them. I scream, "YES! OH FUCK, YES! GOD, YES, DON'T STOP!"

You continue until my body stills beneath you. My legs fall limp to either side of your body. I try to catch my breath. You pull your fingers quickly out of me. My body twitches in response to your fingers. You kiss my clit then raise your head.

I open my eyes and lift my head briefly to look at you. We both smile, then I drop my head back down. You slink up my body, laying your breasts firmly on top of mine. We both have grins on our faces. I bring my hands up to cradle your face as I look into your eyes. You lean in and kiss me. We kiss for a moment, and then you bury your face in my neck. We lie there like that till we both fall asleep.

House Sitting

So my friend needs someone to watch her house for a weekend. I'm on my way over to get instructions and a key from her and her husband, and I can't help but think about their kitchen and the perfect height of their counter tops. I haven't talked to you about it yet because I want to see if they have a problem with me having you over to their house without them there.

When I get there, I enter through the backdoor that goes straight to the kitchen. We gather around the counter, talking about their weekend plans and mine. I ask them if I can have you over for an evening. Like I didn't know the answer, they both have no problem with you there with me. They actually like me with you.

(God, I just want to bend you over their counter and take you!)

"Hey, honey, how was your day?" I say as you pick up the phone.

"Hi! It was okay. I can't wait for the week to be over though. What do you want to do tonight?"

"I don't know. Wanna meet up for dinner then go back to my place and watch a movie or something?"

"Okay. That sounds good. How about Steel Head in about twenty minutes?"

"Yeah, that sounds great. I just left Sindi's house, so twenty minutes will be perfect."

"Nice. I'll grab us a table."

"Okay, honey. I'll see you soon," I say as I hang up.

Twenty minutes later, I am sitting at a table at the restaurant, waiting for you and the drinks I ordered for us. Just as the drinks come around the corner, I see you walk in behind the waitress. You look around her, giving me a big smile. I smile back at you, but the waitress thinks I am smiling at her with our drinks. I look over at her as she sets the drinks on the table, and I thank her. Then I look back at you, "Hey, baby!"

"Hi," you say with a big shit-eating grin and a giggle as you see the reaction of the waitress. She tries to recover gracefully, partially succeeding. I lean over and give you a quick kiss on the cheek.

"I took the liberty of ordering you a drink. Sounded like you might need one. What's going on that has you so stressed?"

"Oh, it is just the stupid people in my classes. They just don't know when to shut up. It is bad enough when the instructor goes off on his own tangents, let alone when the other students stirring things up just to get him off topic. I am going to really have to read my books this semester if I want to actually learn anything."

"Man, that really sucks! I hate it when people do that. I hope the instructor doesn't continue to let that happen. Do you think he knows that he is doing that?"

"I doubt it. He seems to just enjoy the sound of hearing himself talk."

"Do you think it would help if you said something to him? You know, to maybe make him think about it and so that he will be aware of your concerns."

"It might. I don't know, maybe I'll bring it up on Friday."

"Well, on a different note, I'll be house sitting this weekend, if you wanna come stay with me to get away from your roommates."

"Who are you house sitting for?"

"Sindi and Jeremy."

"Oh. They have the house with that low countertop, right?"

"LOL, yeah." I say, giving her my devious smile.

"Hmmm, I think that I might be able to manage a sleepover. Can we go shopping before we turn in for the night?"

"Maybe. What do you want to go shopping for?"

"Well, I was thinking we need a new toy or two."

"And what toys did you have in mind?"

"I'll know when we go shopping."

"Uh-huh. I see how this is gonna go. I'll play. I do like the way you think."

We finish our drinks and quickly order our food with the next drink order. The conversation shifts from toys to her roommates and then back to school. I let her get it all out because I need her relaxed and playful when I take her to the store tomorrow. Plus, there really isn't much I like to talk about with my job. We all just put our heads down and get the work done. No one cares about who is doing what. And that is just the way I like it.

****

I can't focus! I try, but I keep thinking about all the things I want to do to you tonight. Just the thought of you bent over the counter waiting for me is irresistible!

Finally, I get off work and head over to Sindi and Jeremy's to pick up the keys and make sure there isn't anything they want me to do while they are gone.

****

"Hey, baby, I'm on my way over. Is there anything you need while I'm out?"

"Well, hi. Nah, just you is all I need. Are we still gonna go shopping?"

"Well, of course, we are. I'm kind of curious to see what you have in mind for the rest of the evening." (Honestly, I am hoping you want to get a new strap-on for me to use on you.)

"Sweet. I think you'll like what I have in mind, maybe even more than I will." I can almost see the big mischievous grin on your face as you talk about our adventure. Now if these damn cars would move so I can get to you already, that would be great.

Twenty-three minutes later, I finally pull up to your house. You come sauntering out of the house in a tight teal tank top and blue jeans. (Hot, damn. I am a very lucky woman!) "Hi, sexy!"

"Hi yourself, hot stuff!" you say as you lean in to kiss me.

"Mmmm, so where do you want to go shopping for these toys you have in mind?"

"I was thinking Lover's, since your roommate gave us those coupons and all."

"Perfect. I almost forgot we had those." The butterflies in my stomach take flight with the anticipation building in me. Luckily, Lover's is only a five-minute ride from your house.

We pull up to the parking lot and park near the door. I put the car in park and just give you a look that shows my secret excitement of being there with you. We get out and head inside the store. I automatically look at the wall with the strap-ons and dildos. You, however, turn in the other direction. So of course, I follow you to see what it is you have in mind for the evening.

You turn through a few isles until you finally see what you are looking for. To my surprise, you are looking at the suction cup handles for the shower. That just puts my thoughts into a tail spin. You know how much I enjoy making you cum in the shower! But will I get a chance to bend you over the counters? Right off the bat, I start plotting how I am going to work that. I don't think I'm gonna be able to wait until we get to the shower.

Just then, you look up at me from the package you are reading and smile at me. You know my mind is running a million miles an hour. "Don't start plotting yet. I'm not done shopping." (Well, fuck me. What in the world do you have planned for me? And how long have you been thinking about this?)

"Don't worry so much. You will REALLY enjoy the next one." (Mmmmmmmmm, if I wasn't already wet, I am now!) You are like a kid in a candy store. (I may have to fuck you on the drive back to the house if you keep this up.)

"So where to next?" I ask, trying to get you to tell me even the slightest thing that will give me a hint at what you have been thinking.

"Strap-ons . . . " I hear you snicker and smirk as you lead me to the isle they are in.

(That is it—you ARE a mind reader!) "I think I can handle that. What were you thinking? Different size, texture, powered?"

"Size and texture and maybe a new harness. We'll see what they have." I watch you pick them all up, sizing them and feeling them. I can't help but try to guess which one you are gonna pick. I personally think we should go for the purple one, but I'm not the one that it'll be used on, so it is all on you. "I don't know which one I want."

"Well, which ones do you have it narrowed down to?"

"The purple one and the black one."

"What is the difference that you are struggling with?"

"Well, the purple one is slightly thicker, but the black one is longer. They both have the same texture and ribbing."

"Which one do you feel more, girth or length?" Personally, I don't think you are looking for more length, considering my fingers aren't that long and you manage just perfectly.

"I think I want the purple one." You grab it and feel it one more time, then turn to me with a smile, "Yeah, I want you to fuck me with this one!"

My mouth just about drops before I can get a grip and reel myself back in. You just turn and make your way to the harnesses and grab the one that you think it will fit with, which is the black leather with buckles on either side for easy wear. Then you head for the cashier. I, however, make a little stop by the oils and grab a bottle of your favorite scent and meet you at the counter.

I set it on the counter and just smile at you. I chat up the cashier while we check out, then lead the way to the car. I open the door for you then hand you the bag of toys before I shut the door. I can't help but smile from ear to ear as I get in.

"So how long have you been thinking about these toys?"

"Oh, since we got the coupons." You laugh, just thinking about how you were able to keep it a secret for so long. (Two weeks!) I just laugh with you, then I start the car and head to the house.

****

By the time we get to the house, I am beyond worked up. Just thinking about the new toys and the things I want to do to you with them has my heart racing. I pull the car into the driveway and park. By the time I got out of the car and grab your door, you have already grabbed the toy bag and your overnight bag. I walk you to the door, then I open it, looking back at you with a knowing look and a smile. I let you in first so you can drop the bags while I close the door.

You take your time putting the bags down, then you look at the counter top and then back at me with a killer smirk that says I am in for the ride of my life. I approach you slowly, sliding my hands over your hips to your back and ass, never taking my eyes off you. You just lean up against the counter, your eyes begging me to take you.

I lean into you, brushing my lips over yours, then I move to your neck, just below your ear. "I want to taste you before I take you over the counter," I whisper. You just lean your head back, offering yourself to me. My hands work their way over your firm ass as my lips caress your neck.

"Turn around." You follow my command as I drag my hands up your sides to your breast and hair. I slowly move your hair to one shoulder, exposing your neck and shoulder. I take my hand lightly down your back, tracing your curves down to the hem of your shirt.

As I place the palm of my hand on the small of your back, I lean in and let my hot breath caress the skin on your neck and shoulder. I work my hand firmly up your back, pressing you over the counter, forcing you to rock your hips into mine. When I reach your bra, it takes me less than a second and two fingers to release the clasp holding your bra on. Lucky me, you are wearing a strapless bra. It falls down your shirt, but not onto the counter because of how I have you pressed against it.

I take both hands and cup your breasts and just enjoy their softness. They fit perfectly in my hands. Your nipples are hard against the center of my palms. I can feel your breathing getting deeper and more sporadic. My pulse is racing to the point where I don't think I can hear anything else, until you say, "Please."

"Please what?" I say into your ear.

"Please take me. Make me cum. Please, I want to cum for you. I NEED to cum in your mouth!"

And on that note, a switch is flipped in me. I can no longer control the tempo at which I touch you or kiss you. I let my passion take over. I turn you around fast. Grabbing your waistband, I feverishly kiss you as my hands work freeing your body of your remaining clothes. Our tongues dance around each other, twisting and teasing. Your hands forcefully roam over my head, causing so many sensations throughout my body.

That is until I slide down your body to drag your shorts off your thighs to the floor. You assist me in their removal by stepping out of each leg as I prompt you. Once your legs are free of them, I look up at your body with no underwear, which is also a welcome surprise. You just look down at me as you take your shirt off and throw it to the ground. I can see the hunger in your eyes.

I lean in to your left thigh and begin kissing my way upward. I never take my eyes off yours. I want you to watch me. I want to see how you react to my lips. As I get closer to your mound, I can feel the heat radiating toward me. (That is it—I can't take it anymore. I NEED to taste you—NOW!) I jump from your thigh to your clit. I don't give you a chance to move or even prepare yourself for me. My tongue slides its way between your lips, finding the salty sweet goodness waiting for me. Your clit is so hard; I know it is only a matter of minutes until you cum for me. I refocus my attention back to your gaze.

But your head is back, and your hands are bracing your body against the countertop. (What a sight!) So I close my eyes and embrace the feel of your clit on my tongue. Your wetness tastes so good, and I can't get enough—I want more! I work my tongue around your clit, changing up the pressure from teasing you one minute and then taking you to the edge of climax the next. I don't let you cum quickly, though. I want you fully prepared for what is to come, so I slide my right hand up your thigh to just below my chin.

You know what I am going to do to you. You pull my head harder against your clit while you grind your hips into me. You want to cum so bad for me. God, I am so gonna enjoy this! I take two fingers and place them just below your clit and apply the slightest bit of pressure as I glide them to your waiting hole.

It doesn't take much pressure to press them inside of you. You welcome them eagerly. At first, I just press them deep inside while I suck your clit between my lips. You moan uncontrollably. I slowly withdraw my fingers, then just before they are completely out, I thrust them back in. Your breathing catches with my movement, causing me to quicken my movements. I begin fluttering my fingers inside you with every thrust. I know you are about to cum by the way your hands are forcefully gripping the back of my head.

As my tongue dances around your clit, your movements intensify. (Cum on, baby, cum for me!) And just as quick as that thought enters my mind, you begin spasming against me. Your body grips my fingers, then it quickly quivers around them. "Uhhhhh AH . . . OH GOD, YES!" I do not stop my fingers or my tongue movements. I want to see how much you can take. Between spasms, I add another finger. I need to know if you are ready for my new toy.

You welcome the addition greedily. And before I know it, your body grips my fingers tight once again. This time I can't move my fingers within you. I can't even withdraw them from you. I look up at you and see you watching me. I very slowly release your clit from my mouth. I allow my tongue one last flick as I raise my head to smile at you. You grip the hair at the back of my head, yanking my head back, so I can't look away. I charmingly chuckle a little then say, "Hi." As I feel your body relax around me, I slowly pull my fingers from within you. And since you won't release my head, I bring them to my lips to taste you some more. "Mmmmm!"

"I want you to fuck me. Fuck me NOW!" you say in the sultriest voice I have ever heard. You release my head, and I just look at you for a second before I stand up before you. You grab my face and pull me into your kiss.

You hungrily press into me, tasting yourself on my tongue. I reach over to the bag on the counter and quickly grab the strap-on. Your hands work feverishly to drop my pants as quickly as possible.

By the time my pants hit the floor, I am stepping out of them, breaking our kiss just long enough for me to step into the harness. I place the dildo in the harness and position it right over my clit. I look up at you from my strap-on, and before I can even open my mouth to say anything, you turn around and bend over the counter. You arch your hips, exposing your very wet pussy to me. I take a step back and position myself between your legs.

I know you expect me to press into you, but I don't. I take my hands up your back to the back of your neck. I intertwine my fingers in your hair and pull you back towards me. I take my other hand and grab the dildo. I contemplate grabbing the lube, but I KNOW how wet you are right now. I take the head and slide it between your lips. Your breath catches once again, and I know you are ready for it.

"Please fuck me!" is all you can say as you look over your shoulder at me. I take my hand out of your hair, releasing you from my grip, only to trace firmly over your collarbone to your opposite shoulder. I grip you tightly against me, applying pressure to your throat. Not too much though, but just enough to heighten what I am about to do to you.

The second your body froze beneath my grip, I thrust my hips forward, sliding the dildo deep inside you. I feel your pulse quicken against my arm. Your voice is horse and husky. "Ah yessss!" is all you can let out. I am relentless in my aggression. I need to be in you. I work you to a feverish pace, then slow and allow the rolling of my hips to provide you with changing sensations.

(God, I love pleasing you! You make it soooo much fun!)

When I think you can't take too much more, I release your neck and take my hand down your back, forcing you down into the counter. I let my hand settle on your hip. I grip your hip firmly and pull you into me. My body races to meet yours over and over. (Oh god, I am gonna cum soon! I need you to cum.) I change it up again, barring myself deep inside of you hard. Your breath catches, and I know I making the right move. I repeatedly thrust hard and deep. Before I know what is happening, your hips thrust hard against me and begin spasming against my thrusts.

"OOOOH FUCK, YES! Yes, YESSSSS!"

That is what sends me over the edge. Watching you cum because of me always sends me over the edge. "Oh yes, baby, fuck. Yeah! Oh fuck,

I'm cuming! Oh god! YES . . . " My hips thrust into you uncontrollably. (God, this feels so good!)

We both continue screaming and coming until I manage to get some control over my hips and yours. I pull us together, so I can wrap my arms around you and kiss you for the briefest of moments before I take you again. (I am so fucking horny. You are gonna have to lock yourself in a room to get me to stop!)

I decide to take you on the table, so I withdraw quickly from you. The new emptiness in you makes you catch your breath. I turn you to face me, then take your hand and lead you over to the table just off to the right of us. Lucky for me, the table is already cleared. You look at me questioningly. I just smile and push you back onto the table. The height of the table is too perfect to pass up. You fall back onto it gracefully. Your ass is perfectly placed at the edge of the table. I step to you, grabbing your legs and wrapping them around me.

I lean in from a brief kiss, which you conveniently turn into a long, deep kiss. You take my breath away and send me into overdrive. Before my head has a chance to fully start spinning, I grab my dildo and guide it into you. This breaks our kiss, which I take full advantage of. I kiss you down the front of your throat to your collar bone, straight down to your cleavage. (Which way to go, left or right?) Just then, your right side lifts slightly and the decision is made.

I move over your right breast as my arms wrap around your hips, pulling my body hard against yours. I allow the heat of my breath linger over your nipple before I reach my tongue out to greet it. My hips find a constant rhythm that works your body into frenzy. As your breathing deepens, your chest rises to meet my lips. I wrap them around your nipple and suck its hardness. You fight to do something, anything with your hands. I sense you gripping the table, then you wrap them around my back.

You pull me hard into you. You watch me in anticipation of what I will do next. I can feel your need. I tease your nipple with my tongue and teeth. Then I release it to fully look up at you. I rise up slightly as I thrust into you. I can feel your nails poised to dig. You can see the hunger in me. I readjust my grip on your hips, then I adjust my hip movements. I move quicker and roll my hips. And just before you have a chance to cum, I change it up again.

I hear your frustration in your noises. "Don't worry baby, I will make you cum soon. Just not yet. I want to enjoy you a little more first."

And with that, I switch the placement of my hands. I raise your legs up to my shoulders as I straighten above you. Without skipping a beat, you release your grip on me and place your hands on either side of the table. Once I have you where I want you and how I want you, I slam hard into you.

I take my hand aggressively down your legs from your ankles to your hips. I wrap them both just over the top of your hip bones. I look up at you to see your eyes rolling back and your knuckles going white with the strength of your grip on the table. I know it is time. I continue thrusting into you, and I gently slide a hand over the top of your pelvis to place my thumb on your clit. I begin circling it as I apply the slightest pressure on your uterus. (I know how you like it.)

With all of the sensations, you can't help yourself. Before you can even tell me that you are cuming, I can see it. Your body thrust violently upwards with a spasm. I lighten the pressure I'm applying to your clit to slightly extend your orgasm. Your shoulders lock you into a slightly elevated position, so I take my hands and wrap my arms around you and hold you as I slowly lighten my thrusts to bring you down. I know you are probably highly sensitive at this point. I haven't been the gentlest of lovers this evening.

When my hips stop, you pull me tight against you. You are shaking. We stay like that for at least a minute, then you push me away from you and out of you. I'm not quite sure what to think. You just look me up and down, then you hop off the table. You step up to me place a hand on the center of my chest, then seductively, you slide it down to the buckle on my strap on. You work it open, then allow it to drop to the floor. I step out of it, then you grab my hand and lead me down the hall to the bedroom.

I guess it is your turn. I don't think it is gonna take me long. Lord knows I am super sensitive right now. "Whatcha thinkin', baby?"

"I'm thinking it is time for you to get on the bed," you say as you shove me onto the bed. Then you do that sexy crawl over the top of me. (Holy FUCK, I am so wet! Now, you are really gonna know how much you excite me.) When you are fully over the top of me, you linger, just looking at me.

I try to pull you down to kiss me, but you resist. So I let my hands wonder over your body. You just watch me. I can tell there is something going on in that beautiful head of yours, I just don't know what yet. Okay, the anticipation is starting to get to me. "Please!" and before I can say anything else, you lean down and kiss me hard. Then I feel your legs straddle mine and slide back until you are fully pressing down on me. I bring my hips up to grind against you, but you stop me with your hand.

Then you pull away from our kiss. "It is my turn. You can wait until I get there." (Holy fuck is this gonna be difficult!) You smile at me with a look that totally says, "Payback is a bitch!"

You lean down and trace your tongue all around my body, tickling me and arousing me all at the same time, all without touching any of my spots. Just when I think I can't take it anymore, you start moving your hips in circles, pressing into my clit. Your mouth finds a nipple and lingers over the top of it, then you engulf it. The heat of your mouth sends all kinds of signals through my body.

You allow your tongue to dance around my nipple while your body drives me to the brink of coming. (I can't do it; I want to be in control.) You must have heard my thoughts because at that moment, you release my nipple and push your way down my body, dragging your tongue the whole way and looking at me watching you.

You stop barely above my clit, giving me a smile that says you know exactly what I need. Then you dive down, wrapping your mouth around my clit, throwing me over the edge. Within moments of your mouth touching me, I start coming. "FUCK, YES! OH, baby, I'm coming. I'm co—" is all I manage to let out before my breath left me and the feeling of my heart in my throat takes me over. You don't stop or let up; you are not about to let me off that easy. You know how hard it is for me to control my body enough to orgasm more than once back to back.

Before I know what is happening, you have your fingers inside of me, adding to the sensation of your amazing mouth. You are not messing around. By the way your fingers are working inside me, you are on a mission. I don't know how long I can take it. Good thing for me, you know exactly what you are doing because my body answers my own thought. I begin bucking wildly against your mouth and fingers. "Fuck, you are amazing! Oh god, YES! Don't stop."

No matter how good it feels, I have plans, and I am getting sensitive. Okay, enough. Time's up. "My turn" is all I say as I pull you on top of me, removing your fingers from inside me and then spin you onto your back. I quickly mount you and kiss you. My hand finds yours, and our fingers intertwine. When I manage to catch my breath, I pull away from you and pull us both off the bed. "It's not bedtime yet."

I lead you to the bathroom and tell you to start the shower. I leave you and walk into the other room to retrieve the handle from the bag of toys. By the time I return, you are already in the shower warming up. They do like to keep the house cool. I just smile and open the box and pull the handle out. You hear me and open the curtain. (Damn, you are one hell of a sight to behold!)

You smile at me, knowing what I want to do to you, and you motion for me to join you. I willingly get in and position the handle where I know you will grab. You turn your back to me and let the water fall over the top of you. I grab the shampoo and lather your hair up, massaging your head as I do. "God, you know how I love it when you massage my head!"

"Yes, I do." Then I take my hands down to your shoulders. The bubbles on my hands create a nice lubricant for my hands to easily slide over your skin. I turn you to face me, then I take my hands up the back of your neck and gently tilt your head under the water and rinse out the shampoo. You reach for the soap, but I just look at you. You pour some into my hands, which I lather up on your body, and make my way over every inch of you. Of course, I linger on a couple of spots just to watch your reactions.

When you step back into the water, I know it is time to finish the job I just started. I rinse off my hands, then I spin you to face the water. I slightly bend you into the stream and watch you grab the handle. I can't help but feel a sense of satisfaction. I press my pelvis into your ass so I can get close enough to you to do what I want.

I take one hand and glide it down your skin. (You have an amazing back!) I take in every muscle twitch and tense. I stop when my fingers wrap around your hip. Then I take my other hand and slide it under your arm to your breast. My forefinger and thumb pinch your nipple and slightly twist. You arch your back a little so I can cup your breast properly, and I do. I lean into you and kiss you on the back of your neck as I move my other hand down the line of your hip bone to your throbbing pussy.

I feel your pulse race under my fingers as they rub over your clit. I press further down until my fingers are inside of you and the palm of my hand is on your clit. I move my hand in circles as my fingers flutter just behind your clit on the inside. I kiss your back, feeling your moans building deep in your chest. Increasing the pressure of my palm brings those moans right out of you. Now that is what I want to hear!

I pull you up just a little bit with a little pressure on your breast. Then I take my hand up your throat to your chin and turn your head to kiss you over your shoulder. I know you will be coming soon. I notice your body moving into my hand. I let my hand slide from your chin to your throat then to your shoulder. I pull you against me and increase my hand movements on your clit. Your pulse is racing, and mine feels like it is gonna jump out of my chest.

Your legs start to shake, and I know it is coming—you are coming. You start spasming around my fingers and bucking into my pelvis. "OH YES, GOD YES, AHHHHH. DON'T ST—" And with that, I am forced to release my grip on your shoulder to hold you up while I finish you off. I wait until I feel the strength return to your legs, then I spin you, drop to my knees before you, and bury my face between your thighs. My tongue searches out your taste. I can't get enough of you.

It doesn't take long to get you to climax once more for me. With one hand placed firmly between your legs, holding your thigh over my shoulder and the other holding you tightly against my face, you hold firmly to the back of my head and onto the handle. Your nails dig into the back of my head as you cum for me.

When I feel like you can't take anymore, I let up and drag my tongue over your wet body. I pause just below your ear and say, "Thank you."

"For what?"

"For house sitting with me," I say as I pull away from you and smile. You just laugh and kiss me.

Day at the Lake

The day is warm, and the sky is cloudy. Bored, we head to the lake. We arrive at the lake about midday. It's beautiful out here. We change into our swimming suits and head down to the water. As we make our way down, the clouds begin to let loose with a little sprinkle.

As we wade our way into the lake, you splash me playfully. I jog to you and you tackle me, wrapping your legs around me. I gain my balance and swim us out to the end of the dock. We swim and play till the sun begins to set over the mountains.

We emerge from the water and go into the house. We both go into the bathroom. I pin you to the wall, as we pass through the doorway, kissing you aggressively. You grab my top and rip it over my head with an aggression I didn't know you had. You throw it to the floor without a second thought. I grab your top, pull it over your head, and add it to the growing pile on the floor.

I pull you up on the wall and wrap your arms and legs around me. We kiss passionately as I slide my hand behind your head and grip your hair. I tug your hair as our lips separate. Sliding my tongue down your neck, I kiss your collarbone and start my way up the side of your neck. I sink my teeth into your neck just behind your ear.

You moan in my ear deep and sultrily. (God, I love the way you moan! I want to make you moan all night!) I release your hair and withdraw my teeth. You grab the back of my head, pulling me harder into you. I thrust my hips hard against you.

"Take me on the floor," you say in a very breathy whisper. I obey your wish and slide you down the wall to the floor until I'm on my knees. I place your shoulders and head gently on the floor. Kissing you softly, I sit up between your legs, and I glide my hands over your breasts and down your stomach.

Your breathing becomes heavy and forced. It's like you have to remind yourself to breathe. (I love touching you and knowing how my touch affects you!)

As my hands reach your shorts, my fingers curl under the waist band to your drawstring. I undo your shorts, lift your legs above my head, and pull them off. I drop your shorts to the floor beside you as your legs spread and slide down my body. I lay myself on top of you and kiss you hard.

You slide your hands down my back and pull me tight to you as your nails trail down my back. I take one hand down your side and over your hip bone. I guide it between your legs and our bodies as we grind into each other. My fingers begin stroking your throbbing clit. Your hips thrust into me with desperation.

While we kiss and thrust into each other, your breathing quickens, and your moans deepen. The words "Don't stop—your touch feels so good!" manage to escape your lips. I continue pleasuring your clit while I slide my way down your body, kissing and nibbling. My free hand grips your breast, massaging and pinching your nipples.

My fingers start sliding between your hot, wet lips and into your pussy. I lower my body between your legs as my fingers flutter inside of you. I kiss your inner thigh and then allow my tongue to graze over your clit.

You are desperate to feel the weight of my tongue, so you wrap your legs around my head, forcing my tongue against you. You grab my hand on your breast and make me grab you harder. My tongue pulses on your clit. My fingers slide in and out of your throbbing pussy.

Your moans turn into screams of pleasure. I suck your clit till I feel you harden in my mouth. I lighten my lips and allow my tongue to lightly flick around your clit.

You take your free hand and grab my hair. Your body tenses as you begin to come for me. I intensify my fingers inside of you. "YES, BABE. FUCK, YES! MAKE ME CUM!" you scream as your orgasm peaks. I withdraw my fingers from you as I tease your clit with the lightest of touches.

You pull my head up my hair. I, unwillingly, climb on top of you, kissing my way up your body. (I'm done with you yet. I want to please you and taste you longer.) You kiss me and roll me onto my back.

You kiss me again, but this time, it's harder as I pull you into me. You pull back and slide your legs between mine. You thrust your hips into me, making me moan with needed pleasure. You lean down to my neck and bite me. I grab your hair and hold you into me.

You intensify your bite. I grind into you, hoping to break your bite. You take your hand between our wet bodies to my wanting clit. I arch my back as you move your fingers around my clit, showing you how much I need your touch.

You tease me with your tongue, sliding it down my breast. (I want to beg you to taste me, but at the same time, I am enjoying the buildup and your tongue on my body.) You wrap your lips around my nipple and suck hard. The blood rushes from my head, straight to my already throbbing pussy. Your fingers press hard against me as they make their way into me.

You slide into me vigorously with a couple of fingers. I moan louder, welcoming your intensity. You bite my nipple, and then you release it as your tongue trails down my navel. You stop right above my clit. You kiss me, and then you look up at me and smirk. "I love . . . the way you tease me!" I manage to let out.

You wait for me to beg you, but your fingers have already taken what breath I have left. You lighten the pressure of your fingers and all I can say is "Please!" You smile again, lean into me, and take my clit into your mouth.

Your tongue flicks at my clit as your fingers slide in and out of my pussy. I moan and writhe beneath you. (Holy fuck, if you keep this up, I'm gonna cum soon! God, your tongue is amazing!) You wrap your free hand around my leg and pull yourself harder onto me. It's like you can't get enough of me.

You pulse your fingers faster inside of me. Your tongue finds my sweet spot and tortures me. It feels soooo good! Then I feel it, a rush of sensation hits my pussy, I can feel a numbness growing in my throat as my pulse quickens. "YES, BABY, I'm gonna cum for you. YES, FUCK, YES!" I begin screaming uncontrollably. You lighten your lips slightly as I begin coming all over your fingers. Your fingers continue fucking me, and fast.

My hips tense as I grab your head, wanting my orgasm to last longer. You finally stop after I tell you, "I can't take it anymore." You withdraw your fingers and lift your head. I pull you up to me, wrap my arms around you and kiss you with all the passion I have left in me.

CONTROL

I'm sitting at the bar, talking to my friends. I watch the people in the crowd. No one seems to stand out to me; they just melt into one another. (I'm feeling really horny tonight!) I focus my attention on the door, not really expecting anyone to catch my attention. I watch for a minute and see only the same type of girls.

I go to take a drink, and as my beer touches my lips, you walk in. I can't help but watch you. I feel like my jaw must be wide open, but I know it's not. I press my beer hard against my lips to make sure I don't start drooling.

Your long, dark hair flows as the wind comes through the doorway behind you. You're wearing a black, low-cut tank top that clings to your long torso. Your breasts are tight and perky. Where your shirt ends, your short skirt begins. It's a red and black plaid skirt with a thick black belt lying along your curvaceous hips.

My eyes follow you. I take in the sight of you. Your thighs are covered with fishnet stockings, but the rest of your legs are covered with long, high-heeled fuck-me boots.

I bite my lower lip and then regain my composure. I take a drink of my beer and think that I am going to have you before the end of the night!

I pretend to ignore you as you walk past me on your way to the bar. I turn on my stool to watch you from the mirror behind the bar. I catch your gaze as you look at my reflection. Neither of us smile; our eyes do all the talking. You seem to be just as interested in me as I am in you.

Once you get your drink, you turn and walk to the end of the bar with your friend. At least, I think she's your friend. You and your friend take up the last two barstools. I try ignoring you as you seem to be ignoring me. It's not working. I watch you interact with the girl sitting next to you. After a few moments, I know she is just a friend.

After I finish my drink, I can't resist anymore. I order a beer for myself and a drink for you. I noticed yours is almost finished.

I gather up the drinks and walk confidently over to you. You look up at me as I turn to the corner of the bar. I slow my approach as our eyes meet. I say "Hi" as I set your new drink in front of you. You just smile.

"I thought you might like another drink," I say with a cocky smile.

"Thanks! I was getting a little thirsty," you say with a smirk.

Our eyes remain entranced as we talk and drink. Your friend leaves us for the dance floor, but we never notice. I don't want to notice.

We eventually finish our drinks. I ask, "You want to get out of here?" You just nod, and I take your hand and lead you off the bar.

I lead you over to my truck while holding your hand. I help you in, then I walk around and climb into the driver's seat. I look at you and smile as I start the engine. My smile turns into a smirk.

(I knew I'd have you tonight!)

"What are you thinking?" you ask.

"I'm thinking you look like a bad girl who needs to be punished and teased!" I say. You just grin.

After a few seconds, you ask, "How exactly do you plan on punishing me? I'm usually the one in control. But if you think you can take it, then by all means, give it your best shot."

"Baby, you have no chance. You don't know what you've gotten yourself into!"

"Oh yes, I do!" you say as your grin turns to a smirk.

I slide the key into the lock and open the front door. I let you in first so I can shut the door behind us. You take in the room in front of you. As the door latches, I grab your hand and whirl you around to face me.

Stepping closer to you, I kiss you intensely, pushing you to the wall. My hand tangles in your hair. My other hand presses hard into your outer thigh, as I drag your skirt up with my fingers. You bite my lower lip, agreeing to the intensity I began.

I pull your hair, releasing your teeth and exposing your neck. I trace the lines of your neck with my tongue. Your hands grab the back of my head and shirt. You pull me into you hard. I dig my teeth into your neck aggressively, just above your collarbone.

You let out a half moan, half scream. My fingers lighten on your thigh as my fingers reach under your shirt and around your ass. I grip you strongly. I release my bite slowly, kissing you softly.

I drag my tongue up your neck to the back of your ear. I whisper, "My turn for control!" I bite the lower part of your earlobe. You moan deep into my ear. I drop my hand from your ass and withdraw my lips.

I take the hand behind your head and twist your head to the side. Placing my other hand on your hip, I force the rest of your body to follow.

Facing the wall, you reach behind you, trying to touch me. I take both of your hands in mine, forcing them to the wall on either side of your head.

My body presses against the back of yours. I kiss the back of your neck softly. My one hand trails down your arm to the bottom of your neck. My fingers wrap around the front of your neck and climb up till they are just below your chin.

Turning your head to one side, I press harder into you. My other hand falls from your hand to your thigh. I lift up the front of your skirt, dragging my fingers along your inner thigh.

As my fingers reach your pulsating pussy, I force your hand back, and kiss you hard. My fingers tease your clit lightly. You take a hand from the wall to touch me, but I catch your hand again and slam it hard to the wall.

I break our kiss and tell you, "My turn!" You just blink at me and try to hide a smile.

Your breathing is hard and staggered as my fingers fumble over your silk panties. I can feel your wetness soaking through. I slide down to my knees behind you. I reach under your skirt with my other hand. Placing both hands on either side of your hips, I wrap my fingers around your panties and slide them down your legs and over your boots. You lift up each boot in time as I take the panties off and throw them to the door.

I run my hands up the back of your thighs. Your fishnets end at the base of your ass. I cup both cheeks and squeeze. I lean in and bite your bare cheek.

You jump and let out an "Ohhhhhh." I take a hand and lift your skirt. I press my lips to your cheek. You jump again, thinking I am going to bite you again. Instead, I kiss you.

As I hold your skirt up, my hand releases your ass. I slide it, cupped between your smooth, wet lips. I let my fingers curl as I press them deep inside of your cunt.

My fingers find rhythm and flick inside of you. Your moans turn into screams of ecstasy. I smile in my head. (I needed this.) I begin breathing heavily with the thought of your wet pussy around my fingers. I drop your skirt and glide my other hand up your back.

I press my fingers into your back as I drag them back down. I bite your hip through your skirt. You jump a little. I withdraw my fingers from your wetness, leaving you to wonder what I may do to you next. Pausing for a few seconds, I think of what your pussy will taste like.

I slide my body away from yours, grabbing your hips with both hands, and I pull your legs backward. You look back at me. I smile and tell you to keep your hands on the wall. You smile again. Now you are bent over into the wall. With your skirt barely covering your ass, I can see that your pussy is visibly dripping wet, begging me to taste you.

With my hands still on your hips, I grip you hard. I lean in and bury my face into your wanting pussy. I take your clit deep into my mouth and suck as my tongue taunts it.

Your screams fade to muddled words. You begin shaking and your breath is sporadic. I let my intensity wane on your clit, returning my fingers inside of you. They flick in time with my tongue. You spasm above me and begin tearing your nails down the wall. Your pussy clamps around my fingers.

I hear you scream my name. Your legs grip my head. I aggressively penetrate you at the height of your orgasm. I release your clit from my mouth, then I slow down the rhythm of my hand. The silence!

Your legs relax and relinquish my head. I pull away from your pussy, gently withdrawing my fingers. I slide my body against yours as I stand over you. I wrap my arms around you and make you stand upright in front of me. I hold you for a moment until I feel your legs steady themselves.

Desiring more, I take your hand and guide you to the bedroom. I stand you in front of the bed and turn you to face me. I grab your shirt and lift it over your head. I let my hands trail down your arms to your back where I undo your bra. It drops to the floor as your arms fall to your sides. (Your breasts really are as perky as they seemed.)

My hands begin working on your belt. You go to pull my shirt off and I resist. I just look at you and say, "NO!" I continue undoing your belt. I quickly pull it from your waist and throw it to the floor. I unzip your skirt and let it fall to your feet.

As you step out of it, I kneel before you, prompting you to place your boot on it. I reach up to your knee and gently caress my way back down to the zipper of your boot. I lightly grab it and trail my hand down your calf. I raise your foot off my knee and remove your boot. Then I switch knees and do the same with the other boot. I rise up to stand before you.

I shove you to the bed. I wrap my hand around one of your ankles, pulling it to the closest corner of the bed. Now you see the cuffs attached to the sheets on all four corners. I cuff an ankle in, then do the same for the other. As you squirm beneath me, I turn my focus to your hands.

Hovering over you, I begin to smirk. You move back and forth under me, testing the strength of the cuffs. I laugh under my breath, then I lean down to kiss you.

You turn your head as I'm inches away. You try to deny me. I grab your chin with my hand and force you to look at me. I kiss you hard, parting your lips with mine.

You begin to give in, and I release my hand. I reach my hand down and grab your breast. My rough hand feels nice on your soft, smooth skin. I pinch and twist your nipple playfully.

You moan under our kiss. I bite your lower lip and open my eyes to look at you. Pulling away from you, I slide myself down your body. I lean down and barely touch your nipple with my tongue. You try to move so your breast would press against my face, but I recoil.

I look at you and say only, "The more you want, the less you'll get."

Then I kiss my way down your body, neglecting your breasts. You resist moving or grinding your hips under me, but you are unable to control your breathing as it quickens. You moan softly.

My hands trace the lines of your body, lightly tickling you. You quiver beneath my touch. I kiss your inner thigh teasingly. You moan louder and move your hips, so I bite you.

When you relax, I let my teeth recede and my lips soften. I kiss you gently once again till I reach your wanting, waiting pussy. I roughly slide my tongue over your clit to your leaking hole. My tongue rims you, as your moans turn into exacerbated breathing.

I withdraw for a second, then I return my attention to your clit with renewed ferocity. (I want to devour you!) You begin screaming. My hands roam your body—one massages your breast and teases your nipple, while the other finds its way between your legs and over your soft, supple mound.

I drive my fingers in deep and hard. I pulsate and flick vigorously inside your engorged pussy, enticing you to cum. This silences you.

Less than a minute later, your body thrashes below me. Your screams turn to a prolonged "YES." I fuck you harder until you can't take anymore.

My mouth releases your clit with a kiss. My hand slides from your still spasming cunt. I slide my body on top of yours. The pressure of my body calms you. I kiss you tenderly.

I look deeply into your eyes and say, "Now fuck me!" It isn't a request; it is a command.

I release your restraints. You kick me off you and proceed to rip my clothes off. You pin my naked body under yours with a smile.

You lean into my neck and bite me hard, as you thrust your wet pussy against mine. I scream out in pleasure and pain. You withdraw from my neck and whisper, "Payback." You laugh softly.

I exhale the breath I'd been holding in. You thrust a hand between my legs to my soft mound. You smile at the feel of it. Your fingers part my lips, exposing my throbbing clit.

(God, yes! I need to cum!)

You palpate your fingers on my clit. I begin moaning. I place a hand on your back, pulling you onto me. As your body collapses, your fingers slide inside of me. I gasp with pleasure.

You begin fucking me, slow and hard at first, but as you kiss your way down my body, your hand quickens.

Your mouth reaches my clit. My hands fall to the sheets, tearing at them. My moans become screams of pure rapture. I writhe beneath you. I'm coming! My pussy grips at your fingers. I can't hold back more.

"Fuck, yes! Don't stop!"

I pull your face down harder into me. I hold you to me till I can't catch my breath. I release you back to the sheets. My body stills after a few deep breaths.

You climb up my slightly shaking body. I wrap my arms around your back. We kiss. I look at you as you roll off to my side. I whisper, "Good girl!"

THOUGHTS TO CUM TO

I magine us driving up to The Spot. I look over at you, giving you a sly look that quickly become devious. I look back over the road and slide my hand between your thighs, pressing firmly against your already throbbing pussy.

(Just thinking about it makes my pulse race and throb between my legs. I begin tracing my hand over my breast and quicken my breathing. My nipple hardens under my touch.)

I drive calmly yet quickly to the heights of the lookout, pressing harder over you as we climb higher on the ridge. Your breathing quickens as you throw your head back and give yourself over to my demanding hand. I quickly turn the car around and park when I reach our destination. You turn your head to take in the view for a moment, then you undo your seat belt and reach over to me. Pressing your lips hard to mine, you take my breath away.

(As the throbbing intensifies under my touch and imagination, I respond to my need to feel the warmth of my fingers on my clit. I trace my hand down my stomach, hard over my hip bone, and down to my needing wet pussy.)

As our lips begin a dance of exploding passion and entanglement, I soften my touch on your mound and trace my way up to your waistband. Finding your button, I make quick work of it with my fingers and unzip your zipper. I follow your lead and grip the back of your head, forcing you harder into me. My hand slips between the flaps of your jeans, down over your clit, and deep inside your wanting wetness. My fingers pulsate inside you, robbing you of your breath.

(I slide my hand between my lips, wetting my fingers with the wetness I've already enticed from my body. I slide my fingers up and down, teasing myself with the pleasure yet to come.)

You push me away, if only for a second to catch your breath. You quickly duck you head back to the nook between my neck and my shoulder, kissing me and prodding me to make you cum. My fingers quicken under my lack of control. I begin pulsing them in and out of you, hooking my fingers at the last minute when I pull out, hitting your G-spot, over and over again. It's not long before I feel you fingers searching to grip the hair on the top of my head. You grip my hair, and I know that you are about to cum all over my fingers. My pulse races faster than ever. I want to taste you. I want you to cum all over my finger.

(I finally give in and start circling and pressing against my engorged clit. My heart feels like it's caught in my throat. My blood drains from my limbs as I feel my body readying itself to explode. Imagining the pleasure I feel radiating from your body makes me want to cum with you! My anticipation of you coming on me pushes me over the edge. My back arches, my thighs tighten around my hand, and my hips spasm upward. I don't want it to stop, so I ease my touch to lessen my chance of becoming sensitive.)

I imagine you burying your face in my neck as you scream and bite me and as my fingers push you over the cliff and into ecstasy!

Aggression

Coming home from doing some running around, I can't stop thinking of getting between your legs. You don't know it yet, but the second we get home, I'm going to attack and rip your clothes off.

I pull into the parking lot and my heart begins to race with anticipation of all the things I'm going to do to you. I resist kissing you when I park the car, afraid that my lips will give away the thoughts in my head. I follow you to your door, already undressing you in my mind as I watch your ass in those tight jeans. The minute I hear the door unlatch, I immediately step behind you, close enough for you to feel my warm breath on your neck.

My hands grip your hips as you glide over the threshold and into the house. I take my foot and shut the door quickly. As the door slams shut, I turn you and slam you against the wall. My lips find yours with a hunger you never see coming, taking your breath before you can even react. My hands find yours and pin them above your head.

My tongue, with demanding need, tangles with. I spread your legs just enough to welcome one of mine between them. I place my hip against your throbbing pussy and begin grinding against you. I can feel your wetness growing. Your hips roll against me, meeting my thrusts with your own.

I drag my hands down your arms, over your breast, and down to the bottom of your shirt. In one pull, I pull you from the wall onto my leg, breaking our kiss for a split second, just long enough to rip your shirt over your head. However, I don't take your shirt all the way off your arms. I tangle it around your hands and pin you against the wall again, this time with one hand. My other hand feels down your body. The milky softness of your skin entices me to take my time.

I trace over the lines of your shoulder to your collarbone then down between your breasts. Lucky for me, you are wearing your new bra that snaps in the front. My fingers find the clasp and make quick work of it, freeing your breasts to me. I break our kiss to take the sight of you in.

You stand against the wall, your chest heaving. You try to catch your breath. Your lips are starting to swell from my hard kiss. The look in your eyes almost makes me cum. There are hunger and excitement in them that begs me for more!

I lean in to kiss you as you reach to meet my lips, but I quickly move away from your lips to your neck. My free hand begins caressing your bare breast with renewed vigor. (I want to make you cum from just wanting me to touch you before I even get your pants off.) Your nipple rises to meet the heat of my palm. I feel you harden. I begin pinching and teasing you while my tongue caresses your neck.

My breath is hot against your neck. I drag my tongue up to your ear, where I expose my teeth and grab hold of your earlobe. I breathe heavily in your ear, sending shivers down your back, slightly cooling you and making your other nipple perk up and beg for my attention.

Not wanting to neglect any part of your body, I release my teeth from your ear and drag my tongue down to your throbbing nipple. You squirm under my control. You try to free your hands, but I intensify my hold. You want to pull me hard into you and dig your nails into my back, but it isn't your turn yet. I press your body harder to the wall and look up at you. You watch me as I slowly take your nipple into my greedy mouth.

You catch your breath as you feel the suction of my mouth over your nipple. I tease you with a graze of my teeth and flick of my tongue. The heaving of your chest helps the rhythm of my sucking until I decide to devour you. I take my hand off your breast and straight down between our bodies.

I quickly release you from the confines of your pants, and just as my luck would have it, today is a day you decided not to wear underwear. I wrap the palm of my hand over your very hot, pulsating pussy. I dip my fingers between your wet lips and then directly inside your wanting pussy.

Your moaning becomes more and more noticeable as my hips provide a hard-rotating motion to the palm of my hand and into your hard clit. My fingers tease and flutter furiously inside of you. I hear you say something, but I can't make out what you said. The blood pulsing through my ears is deafening. (I may explode just from touching you!)

I tear myself from your luscious nipple to get closer to your lips. I crave to hear what you want me to do to you. "Please, please kiss me," you say in a forced whisper. I gladly meet your lips with mine, sliding my tongue between our lips to meet yours.

I feel your body become erratic, so I know you're about to cum for me, but I don't want you to. Not yet. Not like this. I want you to beg me to make you cum. I stop my hips and drag my hand from your dripping wet pussy. Your hips long for me, begging for release.

Breaking our kiss, I release your hands and drop to my knees in front of you. You quickly unwrap your hands from your shirt and bra, tossing them to the floor. I spread your legs and pull you slightly over my face, away from the wall. I take one hand, slide it between your legs, and wrap it over your hip, forcing you to lift your leg on top of my shoulder. You quickly move both of your hands down to my head, entangling your fingers in my hair. You press me harder into you.

I take my free hand and spread your lips as I bury my tongue between them. (Mmmmm, god, your taste drives me to cum.) My hand slips away from your lips and over your other hip. I trace your hip bone upward. Your body begins to stiffen for me.

I take your clit between my lips and begin sucking it as my teeth tease at biting you. The fear heightens your arousal…you can't hold back anymore; your fingers dig into the back of my head as your hips grind into my face. (God YES! Cum for me, cum all over my face!)

You try to scream but nothing comes out. All I hear are whimpers and moans. The smell of your excitement make me so wet. Your cum makes my taste buds explode with pleasure. I don't want to stop tasting you, but I know I have to if I want to play with you all night. I lighten the pressure of my tongue on your clit and slowly curl it back between my lips. Your fingers release their grip as your hands make their way to my neck and shoulders. Your body starts to shake, and then you collapse in my arms in front of me. You wrap your legs around me and I fall into you.

I can't slow my heart. It is racing so hard I have no doubt you can feel my pulse against pounding against your cheek. I feel you slowly catching your breath and then nothing. I can only assume you are thinking. (I wonder if you are thinking about what just happened or about what you want to do to me.)

I don't have to wait long for my answer. Within seconds of that thought, I sense you tensing to move, then I feel your teeth. You bite my neck and twirl your tongue over my skin until your hear me moan. I tighten my embrace on you. I arch my back into you and lean my head back, embracing your will.

Your hands rub firmly over the back of my shirt, slowly pulling my shirt up over my head until you are forced to release your grip on my neck. For a brief moment, I think you are going to tie me up like I have done to you. You don't, though. You aggressively rip it off and throw it behind me with my bra. You waste no time. You shove me to the floor in front of you. As I fall, you fall too.

Your body presses hard against mine. I feel your legs loosen and unwrap themselves. I yearn for you to touch me, but I can't bring myself to tell you. I want to see what you will do and what you want to do to me.

You look into my eyes for a moment, then you smile. It's not your usual smile. It's more like an evil smirk telling me that I'm going to be screaming very soon. Then you lean in slowly and kiss me, hard. As our tongues dance aggressively around each other, your teeth begin to show. I don't know why you are showing your teeth.

A second passes then I understand. Your tongue pulls away from mine as your teeth close over both sides of my lower lip. You tug at it but not enough to make it really hurt.

With my lip trapped between your teeth, you begin to slide down my body until you hear me protest. I feel the pain begin shooting from my lip down my neck. It doesn't hurt like normal pain; it is actually pleasurable, especially as you move your hand over my thigh.

I try to move my hips so your fingers trace over the buttons holding my pants together. You look up at me while you glide farther down my body. (GOD, I don't know how much of this I can take!) You take your hand and VERY slowly undo my belt, then my buttons, and then you stop. I did not realize it, but I am holding my breath while you are undoing my belt and buttons.

I watch your every move in anticipation. I feel my clit throbbing against your thigh through my underwear. As you see me watching you, you lean down and show me your tongue. I watch your tongue as you lean farther into me, inches away from my hardened nipple. (YES, please lick my nipple. Play with me. I NEED to feel the warmth of your tongue!)

You see what the warmth of your breath is doing to me. You smile, and then you indulge me by wrapping your soft, warm lips around my aching nipple. "Yes, please don't stop!"

You intensify the suction on my nipple and begin tracing around my nipple. Then out of nowhere, you clamp down on me with your teeth. "OH GOD, YES!" And with that approval, you shove your hand down my pants and under my underwear to covet my extremely wet, eager pussy.

I raise my hips to meet your touch. (Your touch feels so good! More, I need more!) "PLEASE" is all I can say.

Hearing that, you release your hold on my nipple. Without looking at me, you say, "Please what?"

You know what you do to me. Your fingers start to press into the wetness between my lips. I can't find my words anymore. All I can do is think about the pleasure—the anticipation of your fingers inside of me. You repeat your question, "Please, what? I want you to tell me what you want."

It takes me a moment to find my voice, but eventually, I do. "Fuck ME! I need you to FUCK ME!"

Without reacting with a smile or a smirk or even a sound, you press your fingers deep into me. I arch my back to meet the pressure of your fingers. You start out slow and hard, but as my moaning becomes more rapid, so do your fingers. "I'm gonna cum. Oh fuck, YES! You're gonna make me cum. Don't stop! PLEASE don't stop!"

But then you do. You look up at me and slowly pull your fingers out of me. "Oh no, you don't. You don't get to cum. I'm not finished with you yet . . ."

I just look at you with confusion and angst. (Not finished with me?) Like you know what I am thinking, you start moving down my body, pulling off my pants. (HOLY FUCK, YES! Taste me, tease me, do what you want to me!)

You finally look up to meet my gaze. Your eyes smile as your tongue stretches out to touch my clit. You dance around its hardness, tasting me, teasing me. You start moaning with the taste of me on your tongue. Just when I think you are going to tease me all night, you wrap your lips around my hardness and suck me into your mouth.

"God, YES! Don't stop. PLEASE don't stop! Please make me cum!"

As if you reached some sort of goal, you intensify your tongue's circulation around my clit. Then I feel your fingers brush against my inner thigh. (God, you touch me like you are touching yourself, lost in a fantasy.)

Within seconds, your fingers have reached my wet, greedy pussy. You easily dip a couple of fingers inside me. You add another, then instead of fucking me, you curl your fingers up under the back of my clit and begin pulsing your fingers in rhythm with the dancing of your tongue.

(OMG, you feel fucking amazing! Please, for the love of God, don't stop whatever it is that you are doing to me!) I dare not say anything aloud. The last couple of times I was close, you wound stop just to play with me. I need to cum. I need to take you again.

Like you can read my mind, you intensify your efforts, and before I know it, I feel my pulse quicken in my throat. The sensation of extreme pleasure shoots like electricity straight to your tongue. My back instantly arches as the fireworks begin to explode within me. The pressure of your tongue makes me crave more. My hands are torn between grabbing the back of your head and making you stay and ripping at the carpet under me. I choose the carpet because I don't want to mess with your movements. It feels so amazing! "God yes, honey! You feel so good."

I know that if you keep it up, I am going to be super sensitive. I need to stop you, so I relax my fingers on the carpet and grip your hair. I force myself to speak, "Stop. You gotta stop, honey. If you wanna touch me later, you gotta stop."

You stop at once. You look up at me and smile, then you quickly withdraw your fingers from inside me. With a light shock from the sensation, my hips spasm beneath you. You collapse on top of my hips and abs. Then you roughly pull yourself up my body. The feel of your soft, warm breasts gliding up my cold skin sends shivers all down body. You laugh at me, then you lean down and kiss me.

Vanity

After a couple of nonstop hours of wild, passionate sex, you finally ask for a break and go into the bathroom. I'm not quite satisfied yet, so I grab the new toy lying beside the bed and strap it on. I grab the warming lube I bought earlier in the week and apply a small amount to the shaft.

As I hear the faucet turn on, I stand up and make my way to the bathroom. You've left the door open, presumably to invite me in. I pull open the door and see you leaning over the sink, washing your face. You don't have a chance to notice me until I quietly walk up behind you. The toy is tucked low between my legs, so you don't expect it when I wrap my arms around you.

You look up at me in the mirror and smile. I greet your smile with a crooked smirk. You know I'm up to something. I take one hand and run it hard up your spine, forcing you to brace yourself against the vanity. My hand entwines with the hair on the back of your head as the palm of my hand caresses the back of your head.

I lean down and begin kissing your neck down to your shoulder. You watch me in the mirror, breathing deeper with every caress of my lips. "Mmmmm, hi, baby," you say as you lick your lips and gently bite your lower lip. (You know how that drives me crazy.) I take a hand gently up under your chin, turn your head towards me, and lean in to kiss you. I slide my tongue past your lips, taking you by surprise. I feel you lose your breath and soften in my grip. Sensing this in you, the butterflies in my stomach swirl into action.

Your breath slowly returns to you as you meet my passion with a renewed energized enthusiasm. Your hips begin to rotate and arch, begging me to penetrate you. I bite your lower lip and pull away from you. Our eyes

---

lock, and I know I'm going to make you cum hard. I back my hips away from you, centering myself directly behind you. You shift your shoulders so you can watch me in the mirror. I move your hair to one side, then I lean down and begin kissing your neck again. But instead of directing my kisses towards your shoulder, I continue down your spin.

I take my free hand over your hip, gliding it with intensifying pressure over your hip to your throbbing clit. (Oh fuck, you are so wet! I want to fuck you hard! I want to WATCH you cum!)

I slide my fingers hard over your clit and into your yearning pussy. I plunge two fingers deep inside you, making your back arch. Your hips press backward, searching for mine. I keep my distance as I work my kisses down your back. The farther I go, the more I press your head downward.

Working you into a frenzy, I feel you are about to explode all over my fingers. "Oh no, you don't," I whisper. I stand up behind you, dragging my lips from your heated skin. I hear you whimper as my fingers ease inside you and work their way out of you. Just to tease you, I allow you to look up at me in the mirror. I watch your expression change as my wet fingers make their way over your throbbing clit.

(Mmmmm, I want to taste you, but I have other plans for your pussy! I guess I just have to lick you off my fingers. Damn.)

Without breaking our eye contact, I drag my fingers lightly over your hip. (I'll make sure to come back to that spot later to tease you again!) I bring them up to my lips seductively. My mouth opens to welcome the taste of you. Your scent rises up to permeate my senses, making me even more excited. My tongue reaches out to meet my fingers, at first just licking around the tips. You watch me taste you, and you begin really biting your lower lip, showing your approval of my actions.

I can't take it anymore; I push my cum-covered fingers deep into my mouth, circling them with my tongue to ensure I taste every bit of you. (I can't get enough of you!) You watch me work my fingers in and out of my mouth as I taste you, remembering how they felt just moments ago inside of you.

I pull them out of my mouth as you release your lower lip and smile. I give you a teasing, playful smile as I drop my hand down between my legs. I position the strap-on perfectly over my clit so that every time I press hard into you, I get added pleasure. I press your head back down and step to you, letting you feel the toy about to penetrate your desperate pussy.

———

I tease you for a moment, then I press my hips hard into you. "OH GOD! YES, fuck me," you let out as the last of my shaft disappears inside of you. My hand grips your hips as I rotate mine. I pulse in and out of your wet pussy. At first, I'm gentle, but as your breathing and body movements quicken, so do my hips. I grip your hair with my free hand at the back of your head and pull you upright. You welcome every inch of me.

(Fuck ME, I can't get enough of you!)

I uncurl my fingers in your hair and trace my hand down the back of your neck and around your opposite shoulder. Gripping your shoulder, I gently apply pressure to your throat, pressing you back into me.

Your body tenses under my touch and thrusts, not because of fear that I might hurt you but because the danger and pounding of my penetration is bringing you to an explosive climax. I rotate my hips, lightening up the aggressive pace and sliding my hand to your clit. My fingers find you hard and ready for release.

Your breathing has become quick and raspy. Your head lies back onto my shoulder as my grip on your shoulder tightens. Within seconds, your hips begin slamming into me in spasms and your back shakes with orgasmic rushes. You scream "FUCK, YES!" repeatedly in my ear. (Pure music to my ears!)

I release my grip on your shoulder, allowing you to bend over the vanity. My fingers gently slide off your clit, over your hip, and up your back in a comforting, loving stroke as you look up and see me in the mirror. My other hand reaches your neck, and I take my other hand down over your ass to my toy. I quickly withdraw it from your still spasming dripping pussy. I adjust it back between my legs and lay myself over your back.

I look into your eyes. (God, they are gorgeous!) I smile at you and then lean down and kiss your cheek softly. Then I press my cheek against yours and hold you till your body calms.

The pleasure I feel from watching you orgasm is becoming very apparent as my wetness makes its way down my leg. Just the movement of my strap-on back between my legs makes me want to cum. (If you touch any part of me right now, I will cum!)

Like our minds are linked, you quickly move from under me. You flip me around, so our positions are reversed. Now my ass is pressed up against the vanity, and you are standing in front of me. You size me up then start working on taking off my strap-on. Within seconds, my toy drops to the floor between our feet.

I watch with anticipation to see what you will do next. (Your lips look so inviting. I want to kiss you! Please kiss me!) Just as that thought comes to me, something in your eyes shifts. I don't know what it is, but it sends a heat wave down my body.

It's not long before you show me what you are hiding behind those eyes.

Despite my need to kiss you, you have other desires. You force me to sit on the vanity, then you lean into me. I lean into you thinking that is what you want but you take both of your hands and push me back into the mirror. I brace myself by throwing both my arms wide.

I expect you to step into me, but you don't. Instead you bend into me, wrapping your arms under my legs. Your lips caress the creases between my hips and mound like they are petals floating on a warm breeze. I can feel the heat of your breath tease me with what is to come.

You work your way around either side of my mound with your kisses until you feel the wetness on my leg. You stop your kisses and withdraw from me a little. I watch you look at my inner thigh for a moment like you are searching for the train of wetness. Then your lips separate, and your tongue reaches out for me. I feel the warmth of your tongue before it touches me.

(OH GOD, the warmth, the pressure . . .)

"Yes, please. PLEASE taste me!"

"That's my plan," you say between the flicks of your tongue.

I lean my head back into the mirror and give myself over to your will.

You feel me melt into you as you trace my wetness up my inner thigh and between my soaked lips. "Mmmmm . . . OH YES!"

"You taste amazing!"

I feel your tongue circle my opening, flicking greedily, searching for more cum. Then I feel you flatten your tongue and apply pressure as you move towards my throbbing clit. (FUCK ME, I'm gonna burst if you stop. PLEASE don't stop!)

You gently wrap your tongue and lips around my hardened clit. Just the warmth alone is—

"AH FUCK! Yes, baby, YES! Don't stop! Don't stop! I'm coming, I'm—"

My body starts to spasm, causing my thighs to tighten around your head. That doesn't stop you. Actually, you do the opposite. You increase the pressure of your tongue and the speed of your movements.

"OH GOD! OH GOD! YESSSS!"

You don't stop, your hunger drives your tongue to lick incessantly, searching for every drop it can find. My body goes limp beneath you. I can't speak. I can't even voluntarily move. I just twitch. Sensing my weakness, you release your mouth's grip on my clit. (Oh god, I am so sensitive!)

You kiss me just above my mound and work your way up my limp body. I can't even open my eyes to watch you move over me. I feel your breath move and hover over my cheek towards my lips. I still can't open my eyes. I feel helpless and euphoric all at the same time. I expect to feel your lips touch me; instead, I feel your salted tongue trace my lips.

I taste myself on your tongue as you slip between my lips, then on your lips as they press firmly against mine. You wrap your arms around me, pulling me tight against you. You stand up, sitting me up with your movement. Our lips part, and you press your forehead against mine. After a moment, I slowly open my eyes to meet yours.

Our Getaway

So we finally get a chance to get away for a week. We are headed to the hot springs in Montana. On the drive there, I am so excited. I just can't wait to have you all to myself to do with as I please. I even packed our new toy. I am finding it hard to contain my excitement. I feel the need to demonstrate my enthusiasm. You seem to be really enjoying the ride, rockin' out to the music and just smiling from ear to ear. I reach over and start caressing your thigh. You look over at me, and your smile changes from excited to mischievous. I love it.

You slide your hand over mine, grabbing it, then you guide me deeper between your legs. You adjust your body a little forward in the seat and spread your legs for me. I begin to have the same mischievous smile as I try to concentrate on the road ahead and what I'm going to do to you! I apply more and more pressure over your mound, causing your hips to start rotating against me. You take your other hand and unzip your pants. You remove your hand from the back of mine and grab each side of your pants and underwear and begin slowly maneuvering them towards your knees. I follow your lead and glide my hand nails first up your thigh till I reach your hip.

You recline your seat a bit, positioning yourself for me. I rub the palm of my hand over your hip to your wanting mound. My fingers gently glide between your wet lips to your clit. You let out a moan that has been building since the moment I started touching you.

I tease you aggressively with my pressure. I circle and titillate your clit until you can't take any more. You begin begging me to put my fingers inside of you. I wait a moment until you beg me again. In one fluid motion,

I dip my fingers deep inside of you, pulsating them as I penetrate you over and over again!

It doesn't take too long before I have you screaming my name over the music. Your body clenches around my fingers as the rest of your body spasms in your seat. You throw your head back and close your eyes as my fingers continue to force your orgasm to stretch out.

Lucky for me, I finish you off just a few miles from the hot springs. You start touching me, making it very hard to concentrate on my driving and the directions to the hotel. You slide one hand to the back of my head, playing with my hair. You know how that excites me. Your other hand traces my hip bone, over my thigh, and between my legs. The heat radiating from between my legs is palpable. I'm throbbing so much for your touch, I think I might just cum without you even actually touching me!

Just as you turn the palm of your hand to cover me, I pull into the driveway of the hotel. You slowly and purposefully press the palm of your hand hard into me, then up to my seat belt and down my hip till your fingers hit the latch of the seat belt. (HOLY FUCK . . . I NEED YOU TO MAKE ME CUM!)

You leave your hand at the back of my head, teasing me, hitting every nerve. I quickly pull into a parking space and turn the vehicle to park. I turn and look at you with a hunger I have never dreamed I would have. (Oh, the things I'm going to do to you in a few minutes . . .)

I reach over, grab the back of your head and pull you into a kiss that can only hint at the upcoming evening. Then, just as quickly, I pull away from you and open my door. As I step out of the car, I can hear you catch your breath. I just smirk to myself.

After a few moments, I hear you get out and join me at the trunk. I have my hands full with our bags as I turn to see you. You see me and take advantage of my disadvantage. You walk around me, turning me towards you with just a look. My back is now to the trunk. You step between my legs and cause me to slightly bend backward over the trunk. You lean into me, placing your hands on either side of me.

I look at you and see that the kiss I left you with has lit the same hunger within you that burns within me. You take your lips and drag them teasingly over mine, but you resist kissing me. Your lips move from my lips over my cheek to my ear. Your breath is hot and heavy in my ear, causing a shiver to run down my spine to my toes.

You whisper in my ear, "You are going to pay for that kiss. Just wait until I get you in that room!"

I just smirk at your comment. That is exactly the reaction I was hoping for!

You push yourself back a step, letting me up off the car. I'm really glad I wore my boxers; otherwise, my pants would look like I wet myself. Between getting you off and you touching me, I'm still surprised it doesn't look like I did. Before walking around the car, I try to adjust my boxers—unsuccessfully, I might add. I try not to make it obvious that I am wet when I catch up to you just before you open the door to the hotel.

We approach the front desk together, and I talk to the attendant. I check us in then lead the way to the room. You have the room key, so when we get to the room, I stop short of the door. You open the door for me, and I carry the bags into the room, dropping them on the couch at the entrance of the suite.

As the bags hit the couch, I hear the door shut and spin on my heels to find you right in front of me. At the same time, we grab each other and collide in what I can only describe as the most passionate, toe-curling, butterfly stirring kiss ever. Our hands explore each other's bodies, tearing items of clothing off as our hands desperately seek to expose each other's bodies.

Within moments, we are both naked in the entryway, and you are shoving me down over the arm of the couch. Your leg artistically spread mine as you lean down over me, kissing my neck. I surrender to you only because I need you to touch me, to lick me, to make me cum, HARD! My pussy is throbbing with only your kiss.

You hold your body over me with one hand, freeing your other to tease and pinch my nipple. I let out a deep, hungry moan at the feel of your fingers. You begin nipping at my shoulders, making your way down my collarbone to the valley between my breasts. Your tongue leisurely makes its way around my breast until you are just below my nipple.

You grab my breast aggressively, taking my nipple in your mouth hungrily. The feel of the pressure that the suction of your mouth pulling on my nipple rips another moan from me. I arch my back, pressing my breast harder against your mouth. Your tongue flicks at my nipple, causing me to want to cum.

"PLEASE, please put your fingers inside of me. Make me cum with your fingers, on your fingers! Your mouth feels so good, baby, I want to cum for you!"

You look deep into my eyes for a moment, flicking your tongue roughly over my nipple. I moan once more, then you drag your hand hard down my side and over my hip, pushing it between our bodies and between my legs. The wetness awaiting your fingers is hot and slick. Your fingers glide easily as I am more than ready and welcoming.

Your fingers press aggressively into my throbbing pussy. The palm of your hand slams hard against my pulsating clit. (I'm soooo ready, but I want to enjoy this a little bit longer. I NEED to!) All the nerves in my body feel like they have been awakened by your passion and desire for me. I soak in your touch, trying hard not to cum too soon.

"FUCK ME, I'm gonna cum, baby!" I feel all the blood rush between my legs, and I know I can't resist anymore. I don't want to resist anymore. The back of my throat feels like my heart is pounding within it to free itself! (Oh yes, this is the one I've been waiting for!)

Hearing me, you quicken your hand and fingers within me. Your mouth sucks even harder at my nipple. (Fuck, YES! You're amazing with that tongue!) "YES, BABY, I'm coming!" I whisper. The spasms of my body tightens every muscle around my chest, causing me to lose my breath. My back arches hard toward your mouth, and my hips buck wildly under your touch. You persist with the aggression of your fingers until my pussy constricts hard around them, forcing you to stop mid-penetration.

You raise your eyes to look at me, finding me watching you as my body settles back down onto the couch. My chest heaves up and down as I breathe. On a downward movement, you release my nipple and just grin at me with satisfaction. I smile back with a different kind of satisfaction. I ease the tension around your fingers, and you pull them quickly out of my now dripping wet pussy. You bring them seductively up to your mouth, licking and sucking on them to tease and taste me.

"God, you are soooo FUCKING sexy!"

You let a finger linger in your mouth as I start to lean onto you. I open my mouth, pressing my tongue against your fingers, licking them and kissing you at the same time. Your fingers slowly drop from our lips as we press deeper into each other.

As you let your fingers drop down to our hips, you deepen our kiss. The passion inside of me is exploding, my need to touch you is palpable. You can feel my need growing with every movement of my tongue inside of your mouth. My hands start to aggressively roam your body, touching you in ways that I know drive you absolutely insane with desire.

You stand up and pull me off the couch, and I follow you over to the bed. You lay down on my back, showing me exactly what I have to work with. I start at your feet, slowly touching them and running my fingers up your ankles and back down over your feet. My hands move up your legs to your thighs, pushing them apart so that I can rub the full length of your leg and thigh.

My touch is making you want to beg me to take you. But you know how much I am enjoying this time, so you let me continue. Your pussy is throbbing with need as I slowly graze it with my fingers. Thinking I am going to keep touching your clit, you arch your back and can almost feel the moisture dripping down your lips.

But I do not continue touching you. I move my hands up to your stomach and ribs and continue my teasing. My body is almost completely on top of you now. You feel my mouth move onto your neck; my breath is warm and comforting. I kiss your neck, your ear, and your shoulder, making my way down to your nipple. I suck it into my mouth. My tongue flicks it back and forth. "God, I need you inside of me. Baby, please. Please, please make me cum!"

"Not yet, baby, not yet," I say.

I continue to tease your nipple with my tongue. My hands roam all over your body. Just when you think I am just going to tease you all night, I quickly drop my hands and slide a finger inside of you. It happens so fast that a gasp escapes your lips. You are amazed by the effect that I have on you. I climb up your body and kiss your lips as I slide my finger in and out of your dripping wet pussy.

Your moans are getting louder now, and your back is arching. You are so close to an amazing climax just when I pull my fingers out and kiss you again. Your body sags in defeat as its muscles relax a little. I quickly lower myself on your body and begin to lick your clit. My tongue is teasing your clit, making it extremely hard!

I take your clit into my mouth just as I slide a finger inside of you. (OH MY GOD!) Your muscles tighten, and your back arches as you explode over the edge of ecstasy. Your orgasm is so intense that you literally push my fingers out of your pussy. I take one last pass over your clit with my tongue just to savor the taste of you, then I climb up your body.

I lie down next to you and reach over and pull you towards me. Both of us are spent. We lie there with your head on my shoulder and my arms around you. What an amazing start to this vacation of ours.

BATH TIME

I wake up, and just lie there for a moment listening to you breathe in time with me. I roll over to feel you, but you have traveled to the edge of the bed, probably because I over heated the bed. I open my eyes to see you lying naked on your stomach with your leg hanging over the side of the bed, and the covers are halfway down your back. I watch you for a few minutes and take in your beauty.

(Hmmmm, what to do with you now . . .) I think I'll be nice and let you sleep a little while longer and go run myself a nice relaxing bath in that huge Jacuzzi tub. I'm so glad I asked for a room with a lager tub. I have plans for this tub when I have you awake.

Slowly and quietly, I ease my body from under the sheet and onto the floor. I look back at you over my naked shoulder to make sure I didn't wake you. You deserve a little more sleep after last night. I think I put your stamina to the test.

As I watch you over my shoulder, and I stand and walk naked to the bathroom. And just because I'm always one for hints, I leave the bathroom door open a crack and turn on the light. The first thing I do is turn my back to the mirror and examine my back for welts and cuts. You sure brought out your claws last night. And I enjoyed every second of it!

First, I turn my left shoulder towards the mirror, and just to the right of my tattoo and just below my shoulder blade, there are four very distinct welts. I smile, thinking back to what I was doing to you last night that made you dig in. Then I turn my right shoulder to the mirror, and I not only see matching welts but also a small blood trail under my name tattoo. (Mmmmm, I am gonna have to remember to thank you for that one!)

With that thought, I turn to the bath. This bathroom is so large that it takes me five steps to reach the tub from the mirror. (Man I'm I going to use every inch of this place!) I bend over the side, reaching across the tub to the side spout and turn the water on. I stay bent over the tub for a moment, checking the water temp. I need to make sure it will be hot enough for you.

When I feel like the water is just hot enough to warm me up and not burn my skin off, I climb in and let the water pour over my hips and between my legs before it hits the tub's surface underneath me. "Oh my, mmmm," I say as I close my eyes and start to enjoy the sensations sweeping through my body.

****

You wake up to the water running and turn your head to where I was sleeping next to you, then you look towards the bathroom. You lie there listening to the water run, then you hear my soft response to the water touching me, and you throw the sheets off your bare ass. The cold air hits your pussy like a brisk wind, and with you being hairless, it tickles every nerve in your clit, lighting a fire within you.

You quickly jump out of bed, grab your phone, turn on your music, and walk to the bathroom. Stopping at the door to slowly push it open, you pose in the doorway to watch me. You watch me sliding my hands under the water over my hip and between my legs.

I moan just as I hear you open the door. I know you are watching me, so I bite my lip. My fingers explore my pussy deeper. I hear the music you chose to play and begin smiling as I open my eyes and turn to look at you.

You are biting your lower lip, and I can tell that you are becoming wet just from watching me. "Good morning, baby. Wanna join me?" I ask as if it were even a question.

You laugh then say, "Good morning, babe. I see you got started without me."

"I thought I'd let you sleep in a little bit. You looked so beautiful and peaceful. I didn't want to interrupt your sleep. I know what I have in store for you today!"

"Oh yeah, and what is that?" you say as you start to slowly, seductively walk over towards me.

"Why don't you join me, and I'll show you."

You give me that sexy smile as you bite your lower lip again and look at me. After a moment, I realize why you haven't just jumped in. You are thinking about if you want me to take you from behind or if you want to ride me. I'm hoping for the latter.

You release your lips as if you've made up your mind, then you step in facing me. (Mmmm, wishes do come true!) You place your feet on either side of me and just stand above me. I smile up at you and start taking my hands out of the water and up your legs as I sit up and start kissing your inner thighs. I purposely pass over your mound, which is radiating a lot of heat. Instead, I pause over it and blow on your clit softly. The heat from my mouth hits you like a well-placed finger.

You quickly grab the hair on my head and make me look at you. That's all it takes—just that one look. I bury my face between your lips. My tongue reaches out for your clit, pressing hard against you. The pulse throbbing through your clit excites me.

You throw your head back and brace yourself against the rock wall with one hand and tighten your grip in my hair with the other. My hands become firmer over your skin as they feel their way up and around your legs. My right makes its way inward, and my left moves towards your ass. As my right hand approaches your pussy, you lift your leg and position your foot on the ledge of the tub, inviting me inside you. I grip your ass and pull you harder on me.

My tongue flattens and presses deeper to taste you. (Fuck, YES! You taste amazing!) "Mmmmm" is all I can say the second the full taste of you hit my tongue. (OMG, I am so going to make you cum just so I can lick you clean.)

Just as my fingers crest the inside of your upper thigh, you moan and rock your hips into me. For a split second, my mind catches what song is playing on your phone, "Skin" by Rihanna. (Hell yeah, it is soooo gonna be one of those days!) I think as I quickly press my fingers deep inside of your hot pussy, past my tongue.

I press them as deep as you can take them. Your moan does something to me, and my pulse quickens. I pull my fingers out to tease you, then I add another and once again penetrate you hard. This time I do not pull them out; instead, I repeatedly penetrate you.

My lips wrap around your clit and begin sucking on your hardened clit. I flick my tongue around your clit, teasing you. Your body begins rocking in rhythm with my fingers. (I love the way your body respond to me fucking you!) I can tell you want to cum for me. Your nails are starting to dig in.

I take this cue and start fluttering my fingers inside you and flattening my tongue over your clit. The dual pressure sends you over the edge. Your hips wildly spasm against my mouth. I want to make your orgasm last, so I lighten the pressure over your throbbing clit and withdraw one finger. (I can't make you sensitive yet.)

You begin to lose your balance, so I release my grip on your ass and wrap my arm around your hips, holding you tight to me. "FUCK, YESSSS! OH, BABE, don't stop, please don't STOP!" Your voice goes from a screaming to pleading. (Fuck, I'm gonna cum just making you cum!)

You ride your orgasm out on my face and fingers. When it stops, you try to pull my head back, but I won't let you, and I hold tight. I withdraw my fingers from inside of you and work my way around your pussy, tasting you till I can't taste you anymore. Then I look up at you and smile. You look down at me with a "why did you stop? I was enjoying that" look. I just smirk up at you and pull you down on top of me and kiss you.

Our tongues tangle and twist around each other's like we've done this our whole lives. You brace yourself with the edge of the tub, as I let my hands further explore your body. The heat of my hands over your back sends shivers up on it. Every muscle in your body tightens. I begin grinding my pussy into yours, creating waves with the water, which adds its own sensation.

I take both of my hands down to your ass and hold your hips as you ride my hips. Our kiss intensifies as both of us begin heating up. You reach in between our bodies and spread my lips with your fingers. I am soooo wet, and you can tell that it is not because I've been sitting in the water. Your fingers easily glide inside of me. The palm of your hand presses against my pulsating clit, and I almost cum right then and there. (FUCK, YES!) I resist. I want to make you cum with me.

I reach my hand around to the top of your hand. At first, you don't know what I will do. I rub my hand over the top of yours, pressing your hand harder into me. Then I surprise you by flipping my hand and shoving my fingers into your lips till they are engulfed inside of you. You tighten around me as our lips part just long enough so we can both moan with complete pleasure.

Our bodies move like we are dancing to your music. We grind into each other with increasing need. As if we really are on the same page, we both start flicking our fingers around as we press in and pull out in alternating movements. (Holy shit, this is HOT.) I don't think I can last much longer, so I start applying my pressure to your clit and curl my fingers inside of you.

As if our bodies want the same thing, we begin cuming together, all over each other. I can't kiss you anymore. I need to scream and catch my breath. I pull away from you slightly, moaning as our lips part. We both scream and moan as we ride out our orgasms.

"YES, baby, yes. Fuck, yessssss!"

"Oh god, yes, fuck me, fuck me . . .," you say as you bite your lip, which only makes me really want to fuck you.

You pull your fingers out of me so you can stabilize yourself. My orgasm eases with the loss of your fingers, but I don't care. Now, I'm on a mission. I sit us up, and with my hand on your ass, I pull you hard onto my fingers.

I pick my heel up and kick on the jets as I kiss you hard. My hips start moving beneath you. My hand acts like an extension of my hips. I flutter my fingers inside of you while my palm circles over your clit. The jets activating the water around us are creating so many different sensations. (Man, I need to get me one of these tubs. This feels amazing!)

You move your hips over me like you can't get enough of me. I want it to last a little bit longer, so I change up my movements and start circling my hips. You know just how to react. Your hips rotate the opposite direction of mine and add a kick by pausing for a brief second when your hips go back. When you move them again, you thrust hard downward into me.

"YES, BABY, FUCK ME! That feels so good! Fuck me." Before you can say harder, I slam my hand hard against you. Your hands instantly cling to my back. The more I fuck you, the more you dig.

Within a few minutes, I have you screaming for mercy. But before you can manage to get the words out, you embrace the overwhelming orgasm and drag your nails down my back hard. You throw your head back as your hands reach the small of my back and let out the best mix of moans and heavy breathing I have ever heard.

I stop my movements when I hear you become breathless and see you become limp in my arms. I withdraw my fingers gently and embrace you. I hold you tight and kiss you till I feel the strength return to your body. I kiss your forehead down to your lips as I lighten my grip around you.

You pull away from me and turn around between my legs. "Now if I could wake up to this every morning, I would be in absolute heaven," you say as you lay your back on my chest. I wrap my arms around you and try to resist my urges to fondle and caress you from behind. I know I have to let your body recover from that last one. (But I don't want to, I can't help it, and I don't want to stop! Your breasts are just begging me to fondle them. Your nipples are screaming to be pinched and pulled. Fuck, I can't help it. But I have to. At least till you catch your breath.)

A few moments pass as we sit in the bubbling water, enjoying the time just holding each other. I have my arms wrapped over your collarbone, and you are caressing my arms, lost in thought. "I can't take this anymore," I say as I take my left arm and quickly move it up under your chin as I grip your right shoulder. I lean in and sink my teeth into your right shoulder as my right hand flies into the water between your legs and covers your clit.

You invite my movements by opening your neck and legs to me. You lay your head back on my shoulder as my teeth make their way up and down your neck. My fingers do not penetrate you; I focus on your clit because I know how hard I just fucked you, and I'd like you to not get sensitive today. Your clit is already hard to my touch. (You must have been thinking about something good.)

You take one of your hands up the back of my neck to the back of my head, holding me down on your neck. You run your nails around my head. (OMG, I love your touch!) You take your other hand down to your pussy and cover mine. You show me just how much pressure I can apply to your clit, then you take your first two fingers over mine and press them into your needy hole.

"Please!" is all you said.

"Your wish is my command, baby." I tighten my grip under your chin and start strumming my fingers within you as the palm of my hand pulses against your clit.

Your breathing quickly becomes labored and hoarse. Your pulse races and pounds hard through your veins. I can feel it on my teeth. Just as I think you might be ready to cum for me, I turn my bites into nibbles and kisses and trail my way up to your ear. "Cum for me, baby . . . I love it when you cum all over me. Cum all over my fingers, baby." That is all you need to push you over the edge.

You turn your head to me and kiss me as your pussy tightens around my fingers. Your cum covers my fingers. Your body vibrates before me. We kiss until your body calms. Then I stop moving my fingers inside of you and just leave them there inside of you, enjoying the moment. Enjoying being inside of you! I relax my arm around your throat and kiss you once again with passion and tenderness.

THE BALCONY

I get up in a fog left over from my ecstasy and stumble to the bathroom after you. When I return from using the bathroom, I find you out on the balcony. I stand back and watch you for a moment. (God, you are so BEAUTIFUL! I can't help myself from wanting to touch you. I don't want to stop. Screw it, we are on vacation, I'm so not going to let you sleep. We can sleep when we get home.) With that thought, I start walking up to you.

We are on the second floor with our own "private balcony," which really just means there is a wall between balconies. The view in front of us is amazing and perfect.

I step to you, gliding my hands over your naked hips. (I love that you walk around naked, I could look at your body forever.) My hands make their way around your stomach as you turn your head to look at me. You give me one of your ear-to-ear smiles that melts me and makes my blood really start pumping. I kiss you on your neck, just below your ear. You close your eyes and enjoy the soft touch of my lips on your skin.

"I love you!" you whisper.

I stop kissing you just long enough to breathe in your ear. "I love you too, baby!" Then I return to kissing your neck. This time, my intention is very clear. I start using my tongue and teeth. The combination sends shivers down your body.

You grip the railing and press your ass backward into me. I feel your pulse racing under my tongue. I press my swollen mound up against your cool ass and glide my right hand down, over your navel to your slightly sensitive, engorged clit.

I start out soft and gentle with my fingers, but as I start moving them further between your lips into your slickness, my palm presses harder against you. My hips grind into you in conjunction with the rhythm of your breathing. Slowly, you let out a soft moan, knowing that there may be people around us.

(Since I have you moaning with just a hint of my fingers around your begging hole, let's see what sounds I can get out of you with my fingers are deep inside of you!)

As the thought crosses my mind, my fingers are already starting to press their way inside of your begging pussy. With one quick thrust, I press them all the way inside of you. You respond to the pressure from my fingers with a much louder moan.

(I want to make you scream with need!)

I flick my fingers inside of you as I pull them out of your wetness and twist them as I press them quickly back inside of you, creating a heat within you and enticing your body to tighten with need. You begin flexing your hips up and down with your increased desire.

Your grip on the railing has visibly increased. Every breath you take is audible to me, and probably anyone within five feet of us. (But I don't care. I love hearing your reactions to my touch!) Just when you think I am going to take you into ecstasy, I slowly withdraw my fingers from inside you with a twist of my wrist.

You gasp aloud, letting me know that you are slightly disappointed that I don't let you finish. That's okay, I have other plans for that throbbing, wet pussy of yours. Before you can turn to show me your pouty face, I drop to my knees behind you, grip both of your hips, pulling you slightly backward and further exposing you to me.

I quickly take my tongue between your lips and begin pleasing you. With just a touch of my tongue on your wet flesh, you let out, "Oh fuck, baby! Mmmmm, God, YES! Don't stop!"

On that note, I suck your hardened clit between my lips and pulsate my tongue over the top of it. I can feel your body tensing to cum for me. (But I don't just want you to cum, I want you to explode with passion and need.) I take my right hand from your hip and over your ass. I tilt my head slightly down and back, exposing your begging hole.

I take two of my finger over my nose and straight into you, sucking harder on your clit. Your body responds with a quick arch of your back and then spasms. You let out an uncontrollable yell of pleasure then quickly catch yourself, remembering our surroundings. That one yell is all I need to thrust harder inside of you. Your wetness makes it easy for me to slip in and out of your now greedy pussy. I force you to cum hard! I can feel your body reacting to every thrust of my fingers and every flick of my tongue.

I continue making you cum until I feel you can barely stand. Then with a bit of mercy, I soften my tongue and separate my lips, releasing your clit from my still hungry mouth. I leave my fingers inside you for a moment until your body can steady itself.

I stand up behind you, taking my left hand back up around your navel, and I pull you close as I slowly withdraw my fingers. I feel your body flinch with the loss of my fingers. I take my right hand and bring it up to my tongue. (Fuck, I LOVE the taste of you!) I make quick work of cleaning my fingers.

When I am just about done cleaning my fingers off, you lift your head just in time to watch me pulling my fingers out from between my lip, with a smile plastered on my face. You slightly tilt your head and smile back at me. I take my hand, place it on your lower back and begin firmly running it up your spine as I stand up behind you. I continue up your back until I reach the back of your neck, under your hair.

Gripping your hair firmly, I pull you up right against me and kiss you hard.

As we kiss, you twist your body to face mine, pressing your cool breasts against mine. You press so hard against my body that you begin walking me backward, back into a chair next to the door. I fall down into the ice-cold chair. My bare ass lands right at the edge while my shoulders press against the top of the chair's back.

You stand above me, smiling down upon me from between my legs. I watch you as you think. Then without a hint of what you plan on doing to me, you fall to your knees in front of me. You lean in to kiss me, so I start to sit up to meet your lips. You quickly stop me by straightening up and pressing me back into to chair. "Don't move. It is my time to enjoy you." You say as your hands pin me to the chair.

I relax and decide to indulge your desires. The excitement of all the things you could do to me quickens my pulse. Without wasting a moment, you lean into me and begin kissing me everywhere except on my lips. You start with my eyelids and make your way over my cheeks to my ears, where you nibble at my lobs. Then you lick the soft skin behind my ears and down my neck to my now heaving breast.

You drag the back of your tongue around my nipple, then you pull your head back a little. You press your lips together and blow a cool breeze over my now wet nipple. My nipple quickly responds to the cold air, perking right up to meet your lips. You slowly spread your lips while looking up at me to see me watching you. Instead of leaning in to cover my nipple, you reach your tongue out to tease my aching nipple.

My eyes say it all. They beg you to warm my nipple with the heat of your mouth. (I need to feel your mouth suckling me! The pressure, the warmth! I need it ALL!) Reading my eyes, you lower yourself over my nipple, wrapping your lips around its hardness. As the sensation of your lips radiates through my body, my eyes show a calm that comes over me.

Well, at least for a brief second, until you intensify your suction of my nipple. Your desires begin to show themselves when you bite me, then take hand from my wrist and grope my other breast with need and aggression. The pain is pleasurable and painful all at the same time. My adrenaline races. (I want to fight you, I want to squirm beneath you, and yet I want to cum for you.) "Oh god, the things you make me feel!"

You release my nipple from the warmth of your lips and start to make your way down over my abs, licking at my skin as you move. You lighten the aggression of your groping hand to a pleasing, teasing touch until you reach my tattoos, inches from my deeply throbbing mound.

Your tongue stops licking as your lips begin kissing. Your lips take on an unexpected tenderness. You kiss the lines of my tattoo until I rock my hips upwards between kisses. It is just the slightest of movements, but it does what I needed it to do, for when you press your lips to my skin once more, you are just above my clit. (PLEASE kiss me there. Please, oh please.)

I squirm beneath you in an effort to show you how much I need you to taste me. You resist, like you want me to draw attention to us and what we are doing up here. "Please, please taste me!" I whisper. You just look at me and smirk as you reach your long tongue down to lick my hardened clit. Then you quickly curl your tongue upward and draw it back between your luscious lips.

Louder, I say, "Oh PLEASE, baby. Please relieve me of my need."

"What need is that?" you ask as if you don't know.

"Baby, you know what you do to me. You know how much making you cum excites me. You know how I love the feel of your tongue on my skin. You KNOW how much I desire coming for you. You know how much I need to cum with your lips wrapped around muy clit!" I say, slowly increasing the loudness of my words.

As the last of my words make their way between my shaking lips, you bury your face between my legs, drawing my clit into your hot mouth. (Holy FUCK, YES! You are going to make me cum so hard!) You steadily increase the suction on my clit and increase the ferocity of your tongue. Just when I think I can't take any more pleasure, you quickly move your other hand from my wrist and between my legs. You slip a couple of fingers under your chin and between my lips.

The combination of stimuli you created sends me flying. My throat is numb, and I quickly lose the feeling in my legs. I can feel the pressure and pleasure building under your tongue and around your fingers. "Fuck, baby, don't stop! Whatever you do, don't stop!" Oh, and you don't.

Lucky for me, it isn't long before explosions start going off under my skin. You flatten your tongue over my clit and just press hard into me as I start coming violently around your fingers. You pinch my nipple, adding to my heightened state. "YES, YES, YES!" is all that I can think to say. (FUCK! I WANT TO SCREAM! I can't feel my throat. My mouth is so dry. HOLY FUCK, you are amazing!)

I can't take it anymore. I grab both sides of your head and force you to stop. You fight me at first, at least until I pull you harder. You finally release me from your grip and slide your fingers from inside me. I buck at the withdrawal of your fingers, then I collapse into the chair. At this moment, I don't think I can even open my eyes.

I can feel you rise up on your knees and lean in to kiss me. With what energy I have left, I reach up to pull you onto me. I need to feel the constant pressure of the weight of your body.

After a Long Day

Your eyelids quickly become heavy after the long day of driving and sex. Before I know it, you are asleep in my arms. It has been so long since I have had a chance to hold and love you that I don't want to go to sleep yet.

As I lie there holding you and watching you sleep, I think to myself, God, you are beautiful! I don't want to ever let you go, and at the same time, I don't really want to let you sleep, but I will for now, for a little bit. I lie back and enjoy the view for a moment, then I slide my arm from underneath your head and quietly slide off the bed so as to not wake you from your sleep yet. I go to our bags and get them situated in the room, then I head to the bathroom for a quick shower.

While in my nice, hot, steaming shower, I fall back into my routine of touching myself. Then I stop myself. I think, why am I touching myself? I have a gorgeous woman lying naked on my bed in the other room. Then I quickly finish my shower, towel off, and return to the bedroom area.

I stop short of the bed and look at you sleeping. You look so peaceful and so NAKED. I really hate to wake you, but I NEED you. I need to feel your skin on mine. I need to feel the warmth between your legs. I need to feel your touch, and I NEED to feel your tongue on my clit. (That's it, time to wake you up. You had enough sleep while I was away.)

I approach the end of the bed, trying to figure out the best way to wake you from your dreams. It is only a matter of seconds before I figure it out. You are lying squarely on your back, legs slightly apart, with one slightly bent and raised toward your side.

I slowly crawl up on the bed from the foot of the bed. When my knees are about a foot from your feet, I begin lowering my body in the gap you have left between your legs. You begin to stir a little, so I pause to see if you'll wake on your own. I'm kind of hoping you won't.

When you settle back into your sleep, you shift your weight a little, opening your legs a little wider to me. Now the opening between your legs is just the right spacing for my body to fill. I begin by getting down to my elbows and knees. I slide my hands out towards your thighs and lower my head directly over your still warm pussy.

I shift my weight and slide my knees back, so I am now lying between your legs. I take my right hand off the mattress and gently glide it over your legs, feeling you and watching to see if it wakes you. As my hand approaches the top of your thigh, you stir a little but do not wake. I smile at that.

It means I truly get to wake you with my tongue. I bring my arm over the top of your hip and gently lay it down so that my elbow is on your hip bone and my hand is over your mound. I take my fingers between your lips and spread them for my tongue. I look at your beauty, then lower my face down to your warmth. My tongue reaches out to meet your clit as I get closer.

I hear you begin to move a little and look up at you as my mouth catches up to my tongue, surrounding your clit entirely. Your eyes do not open, but I sense that you are awake, at least partially. You still do not move under my touch, so I begin sucking on your clit softly.

Nothing! Still, you do not open your eyes or make a sound. I begin circling and flicking my tongue around your clit as I suck. I begin to hear a little movement but still do not see your eyes open or your head move to either side. I continue with my tongue movements and decide it is time I penetrate you.

I withdraw my hand from your mound and lift my arm off your hip. I drag my fingertips down over your hip and the inside of your thigh and yet still no movement. I continue dragging my fingers gently down your thigh to your now dripping pussy. My fingers easily lubricate themselves in your wetness and find their way to your hole.

I take two of my fingers and press them inside your wanting hole. Just as my fingers press deep inside of you to the knuckles on my hand, I see your eyes begin to flutter. I withdraw my fingers, curling them into you until the tips of my fingers are all that is felt inside you. Then I press them slowly back inside of you. I repeat this a few times as I intensify the pressure of my suction around your clit.

I can hear your breathing now. I see your chest rise more quickly and the pounding of your pulse in your clit is coming harder and faster now. I know I have you close.

I change up the movements of my hand and fingers to a more constant pulsating rhythm of my fingers inside you and curled tightly behind your clit. With every movement or sound you make, I quicken my rhythm. Within no time, I watch your eyes fly open. You moan with pleasure and raise yourself onto your elbows to get a better view of me tasting you.

I just smile at you with my eyes and continue intensifying my actions in the pursuit of your juices. (I need to make you cum. I want to taste you again. Fuck, I am soooo WET from pleasing you!) Your body begins to tighten around my fingers. I see in your eyes that you are about to let go and cum all over my fingers.

In no time, you fall back to the bed and begin spasming around my fingers. Your legs wrap around my head, forcing me harder down on your clit. Both your hands begin reaching out for something, anything to grab onto. Your back arches, and you begin to scream in ecstasy! I feel your cum cover my fingers. And I want to taste it, I want to taste you and savor the taste of you.

I do not stop pleasing you until I see you collapse in absolute surrender. I lift my head slowly, easing the pressure of my suction, and stilling my tongue on your clit. At the same time, I stop the rhythm of my fingers inside of you and slowly begin withdrawing them from your now quivering pussy.

I raise my finger toward my waiting mouth. I release my lips from your clit and quickly wrap them around my now cum-covered fingers. As I look at you watching me and smiling in ecstasy, I rise up on my knees in front of you.

"Wow! Mmmm, hi. Where did that come from?" You ask as you watch me savor the taste of you.

"I wasn't done with you yet. I want you all night! And I figured it would only be nice of me to let you rest up a bit before I keep you up." I respond with a grin between licks of my fingers.

You take full advantage of my distraction. You take one hand between our bodies straight to my wetness. Without hesitation, you slide a couple of fingers into my more than ready pussy. You don't even bother with rolling me. "Oh god, baby!" I say as I fall to my hands and knees above you.

Your hips give a pleasant pressure as they rise up to help apply pressure to your hand movements. At first, I feel that you are rotating your hips below me, but as my breathing deepens, I sense your hip change movements into more of a thrusting motion. (I don't know how much longer I can take it. I feel the pressure in me building. I need to feel your tongue!)

I move my hands to your shoulders, then I meet your thrust with my own. "Ahhhhh," I say as I roll us. "Taste me, baby. Taste how much you excite me," I say with a rough, dry, and sexy voice.

(Now that is what I am waiting to hear! GOD, you are fucking sexy as hell when you beg for my tongue with that voice!) You think as you lower yourself down my body. I throw my head back into the pillows and welcome the heat of you.

It takes you no time at all, I feel your mouth wrap around my clit. (I'm so freaking excited that I don't know how much I can take before I cum. God, how I want to cum!) "Oh yes, yes, baby! You know just how to touch me!"

I feel you move your tongue around my clit as you draw the circulation in my body to you like no other part of my body needs to be fed. Everything in me is drawn to you—to your tongue. I press my head deep into my pillow as the spasms roll through me. My hands fly to either side of me, gripping anything I can wrap my hands around.

"AHHHHH . . . ahhhhh . . . oh YES! Mmmmm, don't stop! Please DON'T STOP!"

I arch my hips into you. (More pressure. I need more PRESSURE!)

You understand what I need, and boy do you give it to me. You take both hands around my hips and pull me hard into your mouth. It's too much; I can't take it. I can't. I buck beneath you. Finally, I give in and embrace the waves of passion and feelings washing over me. I fall to the bed, limp. The euphoria I feel is indescribable.

Sensing my state, you let my clit slip between your lips as you raise your head to look over me. I feel your hands release my hips as you press yourself up to your knees. I expect, like every other time, that you would soon crawl up over my body, lie on top of me, then kiss me.

You do none of that, though. I feel you move on the bed at my side. Yet you do not touch me in any way. When I can, I turn my head to face you and open my eyes to look at you. I find that you are watching me, just looking at me with a smile that seems like it was painted on. I smile back at you and lean over to softly kiss you.

CAMPING

Finally, after so long, I get to come home for a little while. It's been a few months since we've seen each other, and I'm just dying to get you alone for a moment. You manage to get some time off work, so we decide to go camping for a few days.

While you were at work the night before, I went shopping for the food and firewood. All we have to do this morning is wake up, pack the car, and head out to the campsite. For once, things actually come together as planned. I pack the car while you get ready, then we both do a mental check of everything to make sure we don't forget anything.

By the time we hit the city line, my heart is already racing with anticipation of the night to come. I can feel the heat building between my legs. I reach over and place my hand on your thigh. You look over at me and smile, but I don't know if you can already see the intent in my eyes or not yet.

The campsite is about an hour or so away now, and I don't know how much longer I can take not touching you or kissing you. I gently lean over and kiss you behind your ear and whisper, "I want to kiss you and touch you all over. I want to feel you tense and spasm around my fingers till you can't take it anymore." Then I kiss you once more and wait for your reaction.

A moment passes, and I can sense your cheeks flush from thinking about me touching you. I start moving my hand over your thigh, slowly reaching deeper between your thighs. I can feel the heat building and radiating from your mound.

Your breathing quickens as you desperately look at me with wanting eyes. I lean over and start kissing your neck as my hands open your shorts. My breathing is heavy on your neck, sending chills down your body. My fingers find their way underneath the waistband of your underwear. (Oh god, fuck ME! I don't want her to stop, but I don't know if I can keep us on the road. Fuck.) "God, don't stop" is all you can actually let out.

Hearing that just makes me want to fuck you even more. My fingers slide over the top of your now hardened clit. With a pressure I know you will appreciate, I curl my fingers inward and press the palm of my hand against your clit. My hand seems to now have a mind of its own, circling and pressing deep inside of you.

"Don't stop . . . make me cum! Oh god, MAKE ME CUM!"

"The only thing that is gonna make me stop is when we have to check into our campsite, Baby." If I am right, the campsite should be coming up in the next ten miles or so.

I began fluttering my fingers inside your very wet, tight pussy. I watch your reaction as my fingers bring you soring into climax. Your hands tighten on the steering wheel, your left leg steadies your hips, and your eyes are unblinking and focused on the road, but your breathing is very loud and labored. Your body grips my fingers with unrelenting greed. I lighten my palm over your clit and slowly withdraw my fingers from inside you, giving your body a momentary reprieve while we arrive on the campgrounds.

You calmly do up your shorts while I go inside to talk to the manager. I look back at you on my way in and see that your face is all flushed. I can see your chest rising and falling with every breath you take, even though I can tell you are trying to get it under control.

When I return to the car, you slap me on the arm and give me a big grin, right before you call me a "Jerk." I just laugh and smile at you, then I show you on the map where our camping spot is. Lucky for us, not too many people are out camping this month, so I had my pick of where I wanted our spot to be.

I have chosen a spot that is nestled in the tree line, just a few feet from the beach, and far away enough from the other campers so we can be somewhat loud and still go undisturbed. Plus, the campground manager told me of some amazing hiking trails.

As you pull up into our spot, I start thinking of all the things I want to do with you and how happy I am to have this time with you. I get out and begin unpacking the tent so if nothing else gets done this morning, the tent will at least be up. You take one side and start putting the poles in, and I take on the other side. We actually manage to get everything put up and organized in a very short amount of time. One would think we are highly motivated.

Once the tent is up and everything is organized and laid out inside, you say, "Hey, let's go for a walk before lunch. I wanna check this place out."

"Okay, that sounds like a great idea." Plus, I have been fantasizing about taking you in the woods for some time now.

The woods look amazing. The path we are on is somewhat cleared of debris, and the trees are all tall and covered in green foliage. To our right, we can see the lake with the sun glistening off the still water.

We hike for about twenty minutes until we come to an amazing clearing with a large boulder overlooking the lake. You walk a little ahead of me and stop just behind the boulder. The top of the boulder is just high enough for you to lean your arms on about shoulder height, so you can just see the lake over the top of it.

"God, it's beautiful." You say under your breath.

I stop for a moment and take the sight of you in. I feel my body temperature rise as I think of pleasing you once again. I slowly walk up behind and wrap my arms around you.

"So what do you think of the spot I picked out for us?"

"I love it!" you say with a smile as you slowly turn your head to the side and kiss me.

Our kiss starts as innocent as a thank-you kiss but quickly becomes heated. My tongue grazes past your lips and touches yours. Like a spark has been ignited, our breathing speeds up, and our hearts begin to race. You try to turn around, but I won't let you. My body blocks yours, forcing you up against the boulder. My hands caress your body, starting from your hips up to your neck. Then I drop my right hand down to your waistband and get your shorts open once again.

As I take my right hand down between your thighs and inside your underwear, my left hand presses firmly against your right shoulder, resting tight against your collarbone and just under your chin. (Fuck, yes, oh my god, how I have wanted to take you like this outside. This is perfect.) I whisper to you, "You look so beautiful in the sunlight, so welcoming."

While my hands are otherwise occupied, you reach up your right hand to grip the hair at the back of my head, forcing me deeper into our kiss. You can't get enough . . . I can't get enough. My right hand briefly comes out of your underwear, making you pause and look at me like "What the hell?" But then you realize I just needed my hand so I could shove your shorts and underwear lower on your thighs, and I would have better access to the wetness between your legs.

You quickly resume kissing me as my hand returns to your throbbing clit. Instead of pressing my fingers deep inside of you, I tease you gently at first. My fingers circle and flick at your clit, then with increasing speed and pressure, I focus more on the throbbing pulse coming from your clit. I feel you begin to squirm in front of me, begging me to be inside of you.

Just when I think you can't take it anymore, I press the palm of my hand hard against your clit and press my fingers inside of you. "Is this what you want? Do you want my fingers inside of you, touching you, pleasing you?" I say hoarsely into your ear.

"YES, FUCK, YES! I need you inside of me. I want you inside of me. Don't stop. PLEASE DON'T . . . STOP!" is all you can let out before you start cuming all over my fingers. Then because I know I can keep it going, I rub the palm of my hand over your hardened clit, sending you into the next quivering orgasm.

I don't stop until you grab my wrist and make me stop. You are out of breath and panting against the boulder. I gently remove my arm from underneath your chin and hold you steady while you catch your breath.

When I look up, I notice that the clouds have moved in over us. Within moments it starts to sprinkle. It actually feels really nice. When you catch your breath, you start to turn around and pull up your underwear and shorts, but I stop you. "I'm not finished with you yet," I say as I kneel down in front of you, pulling your shorts and underwear down and off.

With a smirk that means nothing but trouble, I look up at you and work my way between your legs. You just look down at me with a look of surprise and a smile. The rain is starting to come down a little harder now, kind of like the feel of a soft shower. You arch your back and thrust your hips forward into me. I take your hips in both my hands and begin kissing you. First, your hip, then your pelvis bones, then I work my way down your inner thigh.

I lick and kiss my way over your legs until I feel you are ready for more. Then I glide my tongue up your inner thigh to your very wet pussy. I can see the heat radiating from it. I can smell your sweet, salty aroma calling to me. I let my tongue dance over your clit. The coolness of the rain mixed with the heat from my tongue is driving you crazy.

You quickly kneel down, and with both hands, you grab the back of my head and force my tongue into you. I let it flicker inside of you, twisting and turning with every moan you make. I feel your nails dig into my scalp, pulling at my hair, trying desperately to have more of me. I wrap my lips around your clit and begin sucking you into my mouth. My tongue presses against your clit as I slide it in and out of your pussy. I feel you readying yourself to cum. Your body begins to brace itself on the boulder. Your fingers grip, but you don't pull. Your pussy widens for more of me. But I have no more to give you, so I curl my tongue and flick it inside of you, sending you over the edge.

Your body thrashes against my face, pounding my tongue into your clit. Your body drips and squirts with excitement and pleasure. I need more! I shove you back up against the boulder and quickly slide my fingers into you. Your back arches with surprise and let out a moan of pleasure. Your body embraces my fingers like they have always belonged there.

I place my other hand just above your mound, exposing your clit to me. My lips gently suck you as my fingers thrust in and out of you. My tongue slowly licks at you, taking in all the different tastes. Within moments, you are climaxing again. This time, I cannot control you. I feel your legs go weak, so I just wrap my arm around your upper thigh to try and steady you. Your hands go from trying to grip me to pushing off from the boulder and pulling me tight against you. I continue with my fingers until your spasms subside.

Gently, I remove my fingers from inside you and slide my body up on yours. I feel the chills taking over your body, and I try to cover you with the heat of mine. I wrap my arms around you and kiss your neck. You shiver a bit, so I lean over and get your underwear and shorts for you. Maybe our outing is done for the moment. At least, until I can get you warmed up again.

CPSIA information can be obtained
at www.ICGtesting.com
Printed in the USA
LVHW091328310719
626007LV00009B/168/P